The blue roan stopped long enough to scream a challenge. He held a grudge against the Phantom, and this time he wouldn't run.

Sam wanted to throw rocks. She wanted to shout, to order her horse away from here. But the Phantom wasn't her horse anymore.

The stallions trotted toward each other. Their strides lengthened, flowing into a lope, a gallop. Then all grace fell away.

The horses slammed together. They grappled to bite, to rip, to raise battering forelegs.

Sam backed away from the lunging bodies, *Please let him win. Please, if it's a fight to the death, let my horse live.*

Phantom Stallion

∽ 2 ∾
Mustang Moon

TERRI FARLEY

AVON BOOKS

An Imprint of HarperCollinsPublishers

Library of Congress Catalog Card Number:
2001117946
ISBN 0-06-441086-2

First Avon edition, 2002

Visit us on the World Wide Web!
www.harperchildrens.com

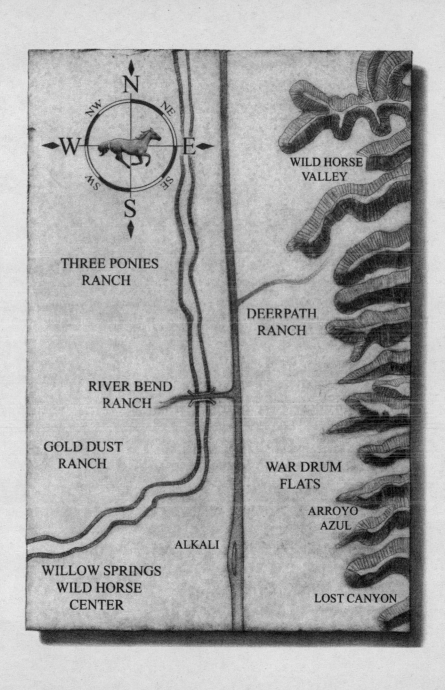

Chapter One ❧

A CRESCENT MOON, thin and silver as the edge of a dime, shone on the lone stallion. With nervous steps, he crossed the river, then picked his way up the bank to the dark and silent River Bend Ranch.

It was midnight. No dogs barked. No coyotes howled, and no night birds called an alarm. The high Nevada desert had lost its daytime heat and every creature slept. Except Samantha Forster.

For weeks, Sam had waited through the night, hoping the silver mustang who'd once been hers would return.

Tonight, after she'd fallen asleep, questioning nickers from the saddle horses had wakened her. Sam had run on tiptoe downstairs to the kitchen. She didn't dare turn on a light or fling open the door to the ranch yard.

Wild as any deer or wolf, the Phantom had good reasons to flee from humans. Just weeks ago, he'd been roped and confined in a corral. Since the night she'd helped to free him, the Phantom hadn't been back.

Standing at the kitchen window, Sam could only watch. What she saw confused her.

The stallion stalking toward the ranch wasn't silver. He wasn't galloping with liquid grace. He wasn't the Phantom and he wasn't supposed to be here.

Fighting to see through the darkness, Sam opened her eyes so wide they burned. She pressed so close her nose touched the windowpane.

Her breath fogged the glass as she whispered, "Who are you?"

As if he'd heard, the horse stopped. His tail switched over thick haunches. He shook his shaggy mane before lifting a head that seemed too big for his sturdy neck. He studied the round pen in front of him and the white house with green shutters on his right. His ears aimed down the gravel road, toward the barn and small pen where a white-faced Hereford calf stared back.

The stallion turned toward the big pasture and paraded along the fence. A dozen tame horses edged closer, heads bobbing as they watched. Sam couldn't hear their snorts and nickers, but she knew the horses were talking.

Frustrated, Sam brushed overgrown bangs back from her eyes. No, the stallion didn't look like the

Phantom, but what were the chances another wild horse would just trot across the river and down the Forsters' driveway?

Zero, that's what.

The Phantom had been born on River Bend Ranch. Sam had hand-raised him from a wobbly-legged foal to a swift two-year-old. Only a terrible accident had parted them. But the Phantom had remembered her and he'd come back.

This horse didn't move like the Phantom, but Sam needed a closer look. She turned the knob, opened the door a few inches, sucked in her stomach and almost slipped through.

When her nightgown snagged on the wooden doorframe, Sam gave it a tug. It came loose with a soft rip.

The heavy-headed stallion wheeled just long enough to see who'd launched this ambush. He wasn't white, but a sifting of pale hair flickered in the weak moonlight as the stallion headed toward the river. The tame horses neighed in excitement as the wild one galloped along the fence.

When the horse abandoned his noiseless moves, Sam blinked. It wasn't his suddenly thunderous running that surprised her. It was his sudden stop.

The stallion glared over his shoulder directly at Sam. Then he struck the fence with a deliberate kick. Amazed, Sam wondered how the collision of hooves on wood could sound just like a dare.

◖◗

"'Catch me if you can.' That's what he seemed to say." Sam waited for her friend Jake Ely to laugh out loud.

Being Jake, he didn't laugh.

He smacked his dusty Stetson against his jeans and leaned against the rails of the round pen. With glossy black hair tied back from browned cheekbones, Jake looked a lot like his Shoshone father. He did, at least, until he squinted against the sun and gave Sam the world's smallest smile. Then, Jake looked like a lazy tomcat.

"Now you've got two horses talkin' to you, huh, Brat?"

Jake was sixteen, just over two years older. He and Sam had been friendly enemies forever. During summer and after school, Jake worked on River Bend Ranch as a cowboy, but he'd never stopped teasing her like a big brother.

"Three," Sam said, jerking her thumb toward the big pasture. "You forgot Ace."

Hearing his name, the bay mustang with the perfect Arab-shaped face, trotted toward the fence of the ten-acre pasture. He tossed his head, his black forelock flipping to show his white star, as he came toward Sam. He didn't get very far.

Strawberry, a big roan mare, darted forward, ears flattened. Ace stopped.

The gelding lowered his head and backed a few

steps, but not before Banjo, Dad's bald-faced bay, joined in. He flashed Ace a devilish look and launched a quick kick.

"Knock it off!" Sam jogged toward the fence, waving her hands.

Banjo's kick didn't connect. He and Strawberry didn't let Sam's shout hurt their feelings either. Both swished their tails and moved further into the pasture.

"Ace, come here, boy." Sam extended her hand over the fence, but Ace stayed back. He looked so forlorn, Sam took his loneliness to heart.

"I wish Ace could tell us why the other horses pick on him," Sam told Jake. "They're just evil."

"They're not evil." Jake gave her shoulder a shake. "Animals have a pecking order. Somebody's the boss and somebody's at the bottom. With these guys"—Jake nodded toward the horses—"Ace is the outsider."

Sam watched Jake. The youngest of six brothers, he'd inherited all the most boring chores at home on the Three Ponies Ranch. When he'd started working at River Bend, Dad had quickly recognized Jake's intuitive handling of horses.

Sam sighed. It had been Jake who'd taught her Native American taming techniques to gentle her own colt.

"Ace looks like he might have lost a little flesh," Jake said. "Beyond the normal cuts and kicks, he's showing ribs. That means they're not letting him eat. I think we'd better talk to your dad."

"Don't have to." Dad's voice came from behind them. "I've been watching Ace myself."

Sam could've sworn Dad had already ridden out for the day. As he moved between her and Jake, Dad's shirt smelled of wind and summer sagebrush, so he must have just returned. Dad worked hard for the bare living the ranch brought in.

Wyatt Forster shifted his weight on one leg, moving with a stiffness that had nothing to do with his boots. Tall, with a face tanned the color of saddle leather, he looked like what he was—a man who'd been a cowboy all his life. As usual, Dad's jaw was set in a stubborn expression Sam had no problem recognizing.

Gram always told Sam that she looked like Mom had, when she'd been a teenager. But Sam knew different. She might share Mom's auburn hair, brown eyes, and way with animals, but each time Sam looked in the mirror, especially when she was mad, Dad's hard-set expression stared back at her.

"We'll move Ace into the barn pen and try Buddy in here," Dad said.

Sam pictured her orphan calf, Buddy, out with the horses. Buddy wasn't much taller than a big dog. For short distances, though, she might be the speediest animal on River Bend Ranch.

Buddy would be fine, but Ace would be lonely.

"We'll put another horse with him, of course." Jake glanced toward Sam.

"Of course," Sam echoed, and she felt her shoulders loosen in relief.

Though she'd been born on the ranch, Sam had just returned home a couple of months ago. After a serious accident, she'd had to spend two years in San Francisco with her aunt. When Jake clued her in about details like this, she was usually grateful.

"He's your horse, Sam," Dad said. "Who does he get along with?"

She held out her hand and wiggled her fingers. Before Dad had given Ace to her at the beginning of summer, the gelding had never been babied. Now he understood an open hand could mean affection as well as food. Even though he could see her empty palm, Ace sidled along the fence toward her.

"C'mon, boy," Sam crooned.

She ignored Jake's groan. He thought she pampered Ace too much. But Ace was a mustang, used to the security of a herd, even if the only other member of that herd was Sam.

Sam considered the horses in the pasture.

Although cattle paid the bills, horses were the pride of River Bend Ranch. In this pasture alone, there were three purebred Quarter horses, a lean buckskin with Thoroughbred blood, a number of mixed breed cow ponies and some young stock Jake and Dad were schooling for resale. And Ace.

Ace didn't want to be a loner, but which horse wouldn't bully him in the small pen?

While Sam tried to decide, the screen door slammed.

"Oh shoot," Sam muttered.

Gram walked toward her, jingling the keys for her huge boat of a car. In khaki pants and a pink polo shirt, with her gray hair coiled into a knot, Gram looked downright stylish. And ready to go.

She and Gram were driving into Darton to shop for a backpack and school clothes. Gram had said Sam had time to feed Buddy her bottle, if she hurried. Sam *had* hurried, but then she'd started talking to Jake and one conversation led to another.

Before she had time to explain she was choosing a roommate for Ace, there was a snort, a grunting neigh, the sound of hooves. Then, pain.

"Ow!" Sam shouted.

As Ace had sprinted away from Strawberry and Banjo, he'd brushed Sam's hand. With a pop, her fingers had bent at a weird angle.

"I'm fine," Sam insisted, but Gram paced toward her at double time and wearing a frown.

Sam's ring and little fingers had already started to swell, but she knew they weren't broken. Biting her lip and keeping the squeal of pain inside, Sam made a fist and showed Gram.

"Just fine, see?"

Gram was too busy glaring at Dad to see.

"You know I love everything that breathes on this ranch—with the exception of that rattlesnake I saw by the woodpile and even he's keeping rats out of the house—but Wyatt," Gram lectured, "I do *not* and never will think a mustang makes a good mount for your daughter."

Gram did love every living thing. Just yesterday, Sam had come upon her fretting over a butterfly in a spider's web.

"Heavens, Samantha," Gram had said. "To free that butterfly means to starve that spider."

Gram had stood watching for ten minutes, before a hot August wind blew both predator and prey into the air.

Now, though, Gram was talking about Ace. And the Phantom. Sam couldn't bear to lose either of them.

"I guess Strawberry and Banjo are out as stable-mates." Sam tried to change the subject.

"I don't know what I was thinking," Dad said. He looked at Gram and rubbed the back of his neck.

"I'm getting used to being ignored," Sam put in, but Dad wasn't in a mood to joke. She knew what he was thinking.

They were all remembering that night three weeks ago and picturing her wild ride away from the Bureau of Land Management corrals. The BLM, the government agency charged with overseeing the country's wild horses, agreed the Phantom was better off free and wild. So while Sam had clung to Ace's back, he charged down a steep rock-strewn hillside, galloping beside the Phantom, leading the terrified stallion to safety.

Dad drew a deep breath. Then, far more than his usual few words came streaming out. "You could've broken bones. You could've fallen and knocked out your teeth or hit your head like you did last time." Dad gave her a hard stare, then closed his eyes.

Sam heard what he didn't say: You might have been killed.

"I'm mad at myself, not you," Dad said. "I shouldn't have let you do it."

"That's the truth," Gram said.

As Gram's voice faded, Sam imagined Ace and the Phantom running across the desert together. Ace might be bullied by the saddle horses, but he had a powerful friend in the Phantom. He trusted Ace. The two horses had matched strides all the way down the hillside.

They shared a wild spirit. If only things could work out like they did in the movies, Ace would be the nerdy sidekick to the superhero Phantom Stallion.

"That stallion hasn't been around since the BLM caught him, right?" Dad asked.

"No, and it's not like I rode him, even when he did come around," Sam said.

"That's not saying you wouldn't do it if you

thought you could." Dad's eyes locked onto Sam's and he waited.

Dad hadn't asked her a question, exactly, so Sam stayed silent. She'd never been able to lie, even about snatching an extra cookie. When Gram interrupted, Sam relaxed, until the words sunk in.

"Samantha," Gram said, "you'd better stay in the house at night."

"I can't—"

"Yes, you can. You'll have homework to keep you busy, soon."

"But I'm a good student. I get my homework finished fast, and—"

"You'll need a full night's sleep to keep up." Dad glanced at Jake, then saw he wouldn't get any backup there. "You're probably thinking Darton High is a little hick school, way behind your San Francisco classes, but you might be surprised."

Sam pretended to study the horses in the pasture. She was really replaying Gram's and Dad's words.

You'd better stay in the house . . .

You'll need a full night's sleep to keep up . . .

So far, they hadn't forbidden her to go out. She needed to distract them before she was forced to make a promise she'd surely break.

"Sweetheart!" Sam pointed at the corral.

Everyone turned to look at the long-legged pinto. Sweetheart was solid black, except for a heart-shaped white patch on one hip. Sweetheart had been Gram's saddle horse for as long as Sam could remember.

"Sweetheart would be perfect to put in with Ace," Sam said hurriedly, although the way Gram's lips tightened, Sam knew she wasn't fooled one bit. "She's never bitten or kicked him. Have you seen her do it, Jake?"

"Nope."

"In fact, I haven't seen her lash out at any of the horses," Sam said, "ever."

"Wyatt schooled that horse to have perfect manners, especially in company," Gram said, looking a little dreamy. "He gave Sweetheart to me right after he and your mother were married."

A bit of the silence was filled by the sound of a crow cawing from a fence post. Buddy slurping clumsily from a water trough took up a little bit more of the quiet. Still, Sam heard the same throat-tightening hush that fell each time Gram talked about Mom.

"I don't have time to stand around and gossip. Sam, you move those horses when you get back." Dad jerked the brim of his hat down to cover his eyes. "There's work to be done, Jake, unless you're scooting off to town with these girls."

"No, sir," Jake said, and Sam wondered if he knew he'd tugged at his hat brim, just like Dad.

As Gram's Buick bumped across the bridge over the river that had given the ranch its name, Sam sighed.

With a quick sidelong glance, Sam checked out Gram. She showed no sign of anger, no sign she was ready to lay down the law.

Sam watched the high desert hills swing up into real mountains to the north. Thick sagebrush made them appear carpeted with green, but Sam knew better. Rough terrain led to the Calico Mountains. Up there, somewhere, lay the secret valley where the Phantom hid his herd.

She and Gram headed the other way.

The two-lane asphalt road ran straight at the horizon, toward Alkali. Too small to be called a town, Alkali had a coffee shop and a gas station. On Tuesdays, the county bookmobile—a library on wheels—stopped there. Sam had convinced Dad to let Jake borrow the truck and drive her there, twice.

Today, Gram drove right on through Alkali.

"I thought about stopping for a soda," Gram said, nodding at the diner, "but we'll get lunch at the mall."

"Great," Sam said, then turned on the car radio. One thing you could say for Gram's old Buick: Its antenna picked up every radio station for hundreds of miles around.

Sam found herself humming along with the oldies station Gram favored. Even if funds were short, and they were, Sam liked shopping. She'd been in sixth grade last time she'd gone to the mall in Darton. From what she'd heard, it had grown.

"Samantha?"

Sam turned. When Gram kept her eyes on the road, Sam knew it was a bad sign.

"I won't lock you in your room at night, but I'm serious about staying away from that stallion. If I catch you sneaking out, you'll be grounded." Gram looked at her then. "I mean that literally. There'll be no riding until you've learned your lesson."

What could she do? Sam looked down and saw her hands shaking in her lap. She put them out of sight, tucking her fingers between her thighs and the car upholstery.

Gram was making her choose between Ace and the Phantom. It wasn't fair. She couldn't stand even the idea of giving up her long daily rides on Ace, but it would break her heart if she never saw the Phantom again.

Chapter Two ॐ

CRANE CROSSING WAS a fine mall. It wasn't San Francisco, but Sam had never adored sidestreet specialty shops the way Aunt Sue did. Crane Crossing was more her style. It had a big department store where Sam got a backpack, jeans, socks, Darton High's green-and-gold gym clothes, and a skirt Gram insisted on buying. The mall's three casual-wear stores were hard to tell apart, but Sam bought two shirts in one and a blouse to match the skirt in another.

The worst part had been looking at her goofy hair in the bright fluorescent lighting that spotlighted the dressing room mirrors. Sam decided she could plead temporary insanity for cutting it to look older right before she returned to the ranch, but it was growing out weird. She needed professional help, but she couldn't ask Gram to pay for a haircut when it was a stretch to afford clothes.

The best feature of the mall was a Western wear and tack store called Tully's. There, Sam saw a split-ear headstall that was a work of art. With delicate care, Sam touched a flurry of feathers hand-tooled on smooth, mushroom-colored leather. How beautiful it would look on Jake's black mare, Witch.

If a good fairy flew down and sprinkled her with silver dollars, she'd buy it. Jake's birthday was October first.

Gram came up behind her.

"Gracious, that's more than we spend on groceries in a month," Gram tsked.

Sam almost snapped that not *everything* was about money. She was glad she hadn't when Gram added, "Wouldn't Ace step proud wearing that on his pretty head?"

Sam could not guess what Gram would do or say next. Frustration made Sam decide that adults—Dad and Gram included—were more unpredictable than horses.

At a table in the mall's food court, Gram chowed down a huge plate of Chinese food but didn't show a flicker of excitement when Sam pointed out Crane Crossing's multiplex theater and suggested they go to a movie.

"Maybe next time," Gram had said as they loaded their purchases into the Buick's backseat, but Sam didn't have high hopes.

The television in the ranch house living room was

ten years old. Gram and Dad didn't own a VCR. Dad watched the news every night, but rarely anything else. She knew Dad did tiring, physical labor each day, but Sam couldn't imagine going up to bed at eight o'clock if you weren't sick. And all Gram did after dinner was read novels and piece together quilts.

They were driving back toward the ranch, when Sam shivered. Something told her the Phantom was nearby. Sam studied every bush moving in the breeze and every dark rock in the distance.

But it was Gram who spotted the Phantom first.

War Drum Flats spread out like a beige tablecloth below them. From the road, Sam saw a basin scooped from the sagebrush and piñon landscape. Gram glanced at where the brush faded to dusty green and gave way to a trampled-bare area around a pond. A dozen thirsty horses jostled for room at the water's edge.

"That's a fine-looking band of mustangs," Gram said. Then she added, "Oh look, there on the ridge."

Sam sucked in a breath, following Gram's gesture. Sam stared past the pond and up the hillside. On a ridge marked by wind-twisted pine trees, the silver stallion stood guard.

From here, he was just a proud outline against the blue summer sky, but Sam recognized her horse. The pine ridge looked so high, windy and far away, Sam wasn't sure the drinking band and stallion were together.

Gram swerved to the roadside. She shut off the

engine, opened her car's glove compartment, and withdrew a pair of binoculars.

Distance made him no more than a sparkling toy, but Sam knew the Phantom by his kingly stance. She could hardly believe Gram recognized him.

"Oh my, it's him, isn't it? Your little lost colt, all grown up." Gram's voice held a mixture of awe and disappointment.

Had she been hoping Sam would really give in to that old idea of out of sight, out of mind?

Gram sat up straighter and angled the binoculars down. Sam figured Gram was studying the mares and foals. Though they looked like miniatures from here, Sam recognized two distinctive blood bays and a mouse-colored horse she'd noticed in the Phantom's band before.

"And who's this, I wonder?" Gram asked.

At Sam's mew of frustration, Gram passed her the binoculars.

"I've never been able to focus these silly things," Sam muttered.

"Take your time," Gram said.

Easy to say. Mustangs could vanish as you stared right at them. It had happened three times with the Phantom.

"Oh, come on," Sam growled at the binoculars. She pressed them too hard against her eye sockets, then held them too far back, so her eyelashes ticked across the eyepieces.

This was important. *Who's this?* Gram had asked and her voice had sounded suspicious.

The first horse to come into focus had tiger-striped front legs.

"Yeah." Sam sighed. She remembered the dun with the prehistoric markings from her visit to the Phantom's secret canyon.

The mare stared across the pond and shook her ears. The other horses moved into a tighter bunch around her, then fell back as she trotted around the end of the pond. *She must be the herd's lead mare*, Sam thought.

Then, the mare proved it. She flattened her ears, bared her teeth, and made a threatening run at an intruder.

"The hammer head!"

"The what?" Gram's dubious voice told Sam she'd spoken aloud.

"That other horse." Without lowering the binoculars, Sam pointed at the heavy headed stallion. "I've seen him before."

She didn't dare say she'd seen him at midnight the night before on River Bend Ranch, but she was almost sure he was the same horse.

His big head, long mane, and stocky conformation were unusual. By daylight, she could see he was the color of jeans that had been washed about a million times. A blue roan.

"Whoever he is," Sam said, "he thinks he's pretty hot stuff."

The stallion pranced toward the lead mare as if she should bow down and kiss his hooves. The tiger dun wasn't impressed.

As the mare attacked, the stallion dodged. He moved like a cutting horse, removing the troublesome mare from the herd as he headed toward the other mares and foals who stood watching, wide-eyed.

Suddenly, he was distracted. Sam had to hunt with the binoculars to see what had made the blue roan swing away from the mares.

The Phantom trotted off the ridge and down a hidden path. He seemed to float toward the herd. Head tilted to one side, tail swishing, he looked only curious. Sam guessed he didn't see the other stallion as a threat.

Full of confidence, the blue bowed his head in a move that puffed up his already thick neck. He pawed the sand, glanced back at the watching mares, then strutted a few steps like a bad boy showing off for the girls. Then he charged.

The Phantom stepped aside. The blue stumbled in surprise, but he didn't fall—just ran a few steps and swung back around to face the silver stallion.

A breeze caught the Phantom's white silk mane and it fluttered around him. The blue's head bobbed in three fierce nods, then he launched a second attack. Once more, the Phantom stepped aside, but when the heavy horse gathered for a third try, the Phantom lost patience.

His ears flicked back and he planted each hoof with determination.

The blue stallion stopped. He lowered his head, and swung it just above the dust. The Phantom had treated him like an unruly youngster, and the blue roan looked ashamed. Finally, without another glance toward the mares, he sprinted away.

Sam saw him go over a hill. She waited. The disgraced stallion had to emerge on the other side, didn't he?

"They vanish just like that," Gram said, snapping her fingers. "Don't they?"

When the blue roan still didn't appear, Sam felt suddenly hot and sweaty. The backs of her legs stuck to the Buick's upholstery.

She'd wanted the Phantom to win, but it hadn't been a fight. More of a scolding. Sam remembered the blue roan's huge hooves slamming the fence in a burst of temper and wished he hadn't lost to the Phantom so completely. What if the blue roan's pride was hurt? Would he return for a rematch?

Sam shivered, though the August heat rippled through the open car window.

The Phantom's band milled around the pond as if nothing had happened, but the stallion didn't return to the ridge.

"I wonder if that was a bachelor stallion, looking to steal mares," Gram mused, "or just a young horse trying out his moves."

"He looked serious, but the Phantom didn't," Sam said.

"The Phantom. Why do you call him that, even though you, Jake, and Wyatt all think he's Blackie?"

"He doesn't look like 'Blackie' anymore."

"That's true, but if he was your colt, he's not the Phantom."

Chills scurried down Sam's arms. Gram couldn't believe in the legendary white stallion, could she? He was imaginary. When cowboys told ghost stories around the campfire, they wove tales about a pale spirit horse that melted through fences. He floated above the ground, outrunning any mortal horse. He passed through lassos and moved with cloudlike silence. But everyone knew the stories sprung from a family of fleet gray mustangs that lived in the Calico Mountains.

Still, Sam wasn't sure what to say. She couldn't remember Gram doing anything more superstitious than crossing her fingers for luck.

Down below, the Phantom lifted his head and stared toward the road, as if he'd finally noticed them.

"He is a beauty," Gram said.

"Then won't you let me go out at night and wait for him? He always comes by midnight, and I promise I won't try to ride him, and—"

"Samantha," Gram's tone cautioned her.

"But Gram, if I planned to ride him, I would have tried to get Dad to adopt him." Sam thought she sounded quite sensible. "I wouldn't have encouraged the BLM to turn him loose."

"Dear, I know you believe that *now*. But if you go out and see that horse every night, if he lets you get close, pet his neck and maybe he even starts to follow you around, the next natural thing is trying to ride him. And you cannot tell me," Gram said, pointing her index finger at Sam, "that it isn't exciting to think of riding through the night with the wind in your hair on a mustang stallion no one else can even touch."

Gram was right. Sam couldn't say the idea wasn't thrilling. She'd probably risk being grounded, for one wild night ride.

"You know I have a soft spot for animals, but I have a softer spot for you." Gram's blue eyes looked into Sam's brown ones. "I hope you never have to sit in a hospital waiting room, head in hands, praying a child will live. After that horse threw you and kicked you in the head, I made a vow you'd never ride him again. And I'll keep that promise with the last breath in my body."

If Gram had been weepy and emotional, Sam might have reminded her that he hadn't hurt her on purpose. She'd fallen from Blackie, and he'd been running away in fright when his hoof grazed her head. But Gram was speaking in a level tone, without a hint of tears. Sam knew, today, she couldn't win.

Sam looked down the two-lane asphalt road ahead and saw a car coming toward them. It glittered like glass and that was the hint that told her it was Linc Slocum's big beige Cadillac.

The city slicker had purchased everything from a cattle ranch to spurs, trying to fulfill his dream of being a cowboy. Still, he had the Cadillac washed every day by a ranch hand, instead of driving a car coated with desert dust like a real cowboy would.

Slocum didn't mind folks calling him a show-off or frowning at the rodeo trophy belt buckle he'd purchased, not won. The thing that did drive Slocum crazy was his inability to buy the best Western trophy of all: the Phantom.

Two weeks ago, instead of putting the Phantom up for adoption, the BLM had freed him. The government agency was protecting the Phantom, hoping the stallion would mate with wild mares and improve the mustang breed.

But why tempt fate? Sam didn't want Linc Slocum to even see the Phantom.

"Gram, go," Sam said. "Here comes Linc Slocum and I think it would be really bad if he saw the—uh, Blackie."

It took Gram a minute to remember Sam's conflict with Slocum, but then she revved up the Buick's engine. She looked back carefully before pulling from the roadside onto the street.

Run, boy, run. Sam stared at the stallion and sent her thoughts winging toward him. *Go, now.* The Phantom circled his mares at a nervous trot and the tiger dun followed.

Sam stared down the road. Slocum's Cadillac was gaining on them, about two city blocks away. If he looked over the edge now, he'd see the mustangs for sure.

Gram pulled onto the road, and still the horses stayed clustered by the pond. Sam had to do something.

She'd never uttered the stallion's secret name within human hearing. Jake had taught her techniques from generations of Shoshone horse tamers. He said a secret name bonded one horse to one rider. Sam could see no harm in thinking the name, so she did.

Run, Zanzibar, run.

As if she'd screamed the words, the stallion bolted. The tiger dun wheeled away from the water and darted toward the hills. In a tight knot the other mares followed. The Phantom circled behind, nipping their haunches, pushing with his mighty chest until the last mare crested the hill.

Just like the blue roan, the horses vanished. A plume of dust rose, then drifted on the desert air.

Chapter Three ௸

$\mathcal{L}$INC SLOCUM MADE sure Gram stopped. He stepped into the street and waved his arms frantically.

By the time Gram pulled back onto the shoulder and halted directly across the street from him, she and Sam could see his emergency was minor. Slocum was squatted next to his Cadillac's rear tire and it wasn't even flat.

Sam shook her head in disgust. In San Francisco, the crime rate was high. People were suspicious. They'd see this for what it was: a setup.

In rural Nevada, folks lived by the code of the West, which said you *had* to be neighborly to everyone. That included a villain like Linc Slocum.

Even the U.S. government agreed Slocum was bad news. The BLM had denied Slocum the right to adopt a mustang. Slocum had admitted he hadn't reported the harassment of a wild horse. That was grounds for denial.

What Slocum had really done was worse. With a truck, he'd chased the Phantom for miles. As the stallion began to tire, Slocum roped him. The stallion might have won the tug-of-war, except that the end of the rope was tied to a barrel full of concrete. Only luck kept the Phantom's neck from snapping when he hit the end of the rope. The stallion fought and bucked and lunged until, at last, the rope broke.

Though local ranchers scorned Slocum, no one could confirm what had happened. They *believed* it happened, but no one had seen it with his own eyes.

Now, Slocum looked at Sam and Gram and waved.

Slocum was a big man, at least six feet tall and egg shaped. His hair was slicked back, flat and shiny. His jeans and plaid shirt pulled tight as he squatted. He probably hoped the position made him look like a cowboy ready to brand a calf. But it didn't.

Slocum flashed his toothpaste-commercial grin as he called across the road.

"If it ain't my two favorite ladies come to rescue me." He gestured with a little metal tool. "This tire keeps on going flat, so I'm checking how much air I've got."

Slocum stood, wedged the tool into his pocket, and walked across the road. He jingled as he walked and Sam wondered why he wore spurs to drive a car.

Slocum put both hands on the Buick's driver-side window frame. Gram drew back a little.

"Hi there," Slocum said. His fake smile flashed

across to Sam, but it showed a little confusion. "Haven't seen you for a month of Sundays, little lady. How long's it been?"

Slocum's outdated Western expressions made even his own cowboys laugh, but he didn't care.

Sam shrugged as if she couldn't remember either.

Slocum kept a hand on Gram's window frame as he glanced back toward his polished Cadillac. "It's time to replace that car. I don't like wondering if I can make it all the way home."

Sam pictured Slocum trying to walk the ten miles from here to Gold Dust Ranch in his high-heeled boots. Then she imagined him squeezing into Gram's car.

Oh no. No way. Sam wished Gram could read her brain waves as well as horses could. Gram glanced in the backseat at the bags of new clothes. Sam was afraid Gram was about to ask her to move them into the trunk.

"That tire does look low," Gram sounded as if, for the first time in her life, neighborliness would be a chore.

"If you could follow me back to the ranch just to make sure I get there," Slocum said, "I'd be awful grateful."

Did Linc Slocum hear Gram sigh in relief? Compared to being his chauffeur, it seemed like a fine idea.

"I'd be glad to do that, Linc," Gram said, "just so long as I get home in time to start dinner."

Uncertainty about his car didn't slow Slocum

down. At first, Gram tried to keep up, then she let him pull away.

"Imagine replacing a car because its tires are old." Gram chuckled, but she didn't sound amused.

Since Sam had returned home, Dad and Gram had made her sit through discussions of ranch finances. Sam found the talks boring, but she understood why Linc's remark made Gram envious.

They drove another couple miles.

"We wanted to spend more," Gram said suddenly.

"What?"

"On your school clothes."

"Don't worry about it, Gram. Really." Sam patted Gram's arm, hoping her frown would disappear. "I haven't even unpacked the box of stuff Aunt Sue mailed me."

Sam had left most of her school clothes in her room in San Francisco. Since the box had arrived, the weather had been stifling hot. The idea of trying on wool slacks and pullover sweaters was repulsive. "Besides," Sam said, just in case Gram was thinking that would be a good way to end the day, "clothes aren't a big deal to me."

Gram looked skeptical. "When you're starting your first year of high school, clothes are important."

Was Gram trying to make her feel worse? Sam didn't have time to worry about clothes or money, when the blue roan and the Phantom might harm each other. But Gram wouldn't stop.

"There's a darn good reason we're careful with our money." Gram made a hushing movement when Sam tried to interrupt. "We won't make much from fall cattle sales. Drought means sparse grass and that translates into thinner cattle. And, of course, we get paid by the pound."

Sam cringed inside, but she didn't say a word.

If her orphan calf, Buddy, hadn't stepped into a pool of quicksand and had to be rescued, she'd be out on River Bend lands right now, fattening for market.

Sam's stomach twisted with nausea.

It could still happen. Sam couldn't make herself ask Dad if she could keep Buddy as a pet.

"And of course there's the BLM," Gram went on. "It takes twenty acres to support a cow and her calf, so we have to use federal land to graze our stock. When they raise grazing fees for every cow who roams on land that's not strictly River Bend—" Gram stopped talking. "I'm sorry, honey. It's useless to complain and worse to be angry at Linc Slocum for having money."

Linc turned the Cadillac toward huge ornate iron gates. Beyond, Sam saw acres of pastures that looked almost neon green compared to the endless expanses of gray-green. In a desert state, water to keep things green didn't come cheap.

"I wonder how he made so much money," Sam mused.

"Honey, it wouldn't be polite to ask."

Sam had hoped they'd see Slocum to his gate and leave, but as the big iron gates swung wide via remote control, Slocum beckoned them to follow. Gram did.

The last time Sam had been on this property, the ranch had belonged to the Kenworthys. Lila and Jed Kenworthy were nice people with a daughter Jennifer, who was about her age. Sam hadn't gone to school with her, though, because Jennifer's mother had taught her at home.

Gram's Buick rolled through the soaring iron gates and into a Western wonderland. Flowers flanked the freshly paved road. White wooden fences marked off velvety pastures full of Black Angus and Dutch belted cattle, animals that were black in front and back, with a wide band of white fur around their middles.

Gram nodded at the Dutch belted cattle.

"Linc told your dad he bought a hundred head of them, because they reminded Rachel of Oreo cookies," Gram said.

Rachel, Sam remembered, was Slocum's daughter. He'd mentioned buying her a dressage horse, though Jake had told Sam that Rachel was more interested in MTV and the latest color of nail polish than she was horses.

There were plenty of horses on Slocum's ranch. A herd of Shetland ponies scampered along the fence on the left. On the right, Sam saw a dozen lean-limbed horses that had to be racing Appaloosas.

In the last pasture, a dozen assorted horses left off

grazing. Tails swishing, grass dripping from their muzzles, they watched the car drive by. Sam would bet they were off-duty cow horses.

A line of redwood hitching posts, polished and fitted with brass tie rings, led them further up the driveway.

Sam finally recognized a round pen similar to the one at home. An animal moved inside, but she couldn't see through the closely placed rails.

What Sam did not recognize was the structure up ahead. It was something she couldn't possibly have forgotten.

The road arrowed into a half circle marked off for parking. The ranch house Sam remembered had vanished, and a hill rose abruptly out of level ground. Atop the hill stood a mansion that looked like it belonged on a Southern plantation, not a ranch.

Before Sam had a chance to comprehend the sight, Slocum appeared at Gram's window once more.

"You're a horsewoman, Grace," he said. "Would you mind looking at something and telling me what you think?"

Neither Gram nor Sam could resist such an invitation.

Slocum led the way to the round corral, opened the gate, and nodded them in before closing it.

The mare was the red of a summer sunset. No more than fourteen hands high, she moved with deerlike quickness, trotting away. Her hooves floated in a haze of dust. With her shoulder pressed to the fence at the far side of the pen, the mare curved her neck and studied the unfamiliar humans.

Slocum strolled toward the horse. Her sorrel skin shivered as if shaking off flies. When Slocum reached for her halter, the mare moved off. That's when Sam noticed her flank was stamped with the River Bend brand.

"Is she ours?" Sam whispered.

Gram shook her head. "She was, but Wyatt sold Kitty to Jed Kenworthy right after"—Gram drew a breath—"your accident."

Sam's hands covered her stomach as if she'd been socked. *Princess Kitty*. No wonder the mare looked familiar. She was Blackie's mother.

Why had Dad sold Kitty? Why would he sell a Quarter horse mare with super cow sense, who produced beautiful foals?

Right after your accident, Gram had said. She couldn't mean Dad had sold Kitty because she was Blackie's dam, could she?

Slocum quickened his steps, then he jogged, but the sorrel stayed a few steps ahead.

"The marks on her haunches, Linc?" Gram called to Slocum. "Is that what you wanted me to see?"

Puffing and out of breath, Slocum returned to stand beside them. "Yeah," he said. "What do you think?"

Sam recognized the marks at once. They were the

same nips and teeth rakings she saw on Ace.

"Do you think they're claw scratches from a cougar?" Slocum asked.

"Oh no," Gram said. "They're bites from another horse."

"That's what Kenworthy said, too, but it's strange. The mare was gone from the saddle horse pasture yesterday morning, then we heard her neighing from outside the front gate." Slocum pointed toward the fancy iron entrance.

Sam knew it was rare for a captive horse to leave guaranteed food and water, but it wasn't unheard of.

"We did turn out range horses for a few years, and I've no doubt they ran with the mustangs," Gram said. "Maybe Kitty just took it into her head to try it again."

"That doesn't explain the bites, now, does it?" Slocum's tone turned mocking and his eyebrows arched.

He clearly had an explanation in mind, but Gram refused to play along.

"I guess you'll never know," Gram said.

"But I do know. Kenworthy found strange hoof-prints, *unshod* hoofprints, in the flower beds along the road." With a triumphant laugh, Slocum turned toward Sam. "The Phantom came in here and tried to steal her."

"No, he didn't," Sam snapped. At Gram's sharp intake of breath, Sam made a polite addition. "I'm sure you must be mistaken, Mr. Slocum."

"I tend to agree, Linc." Gram shook her head. "I've lived here all my life. In sixty-five years, we've never had a wild stallion up near the house, unless we roped him and brought him in."

Oh yes, we have. Sam thought of the blue roan. He'd been after the Phantom's mares today. And she'd seen him right outside the kitchen door, but if she said that, she'd be grounded.

"I hate to contradict a lady," Slocum said. "But I know for a fact that white stud's been on River Bend property."

Sam suspected Slocum of lurking on the ridge above the River Bend at night, spying with binoculars. But Sam kept her lips pressed together hard, and lagged behind Gram and Slocum as they left the round pen.

Gram was quiet, until they reached the Buick.

"If you're talking about the gray mustang," Gram said, once more refusing to call him the Phantom, "I don't think he's been any closer than the river. Am I right, Samantha?"

"Absolutely." Sam tightened her hands into fists.

"Well, we'll see. We'll certainly see." Slocum nodded four times. "I've got expensive bloodstock on this ranch. My herd of Shetlands, Quarter horses, a couple Thoroughbreds, a Saddlebred, and a dressage horse, just to name a few." Slocum let out a breath as if listing his possessions wearied him.

"Kitty's a good cow horse. You're lucky she found her way back," Gram said, sympathizing. "I know she was one of Wyatt's favorites."

Slocum dismissed the mare with a wave of his hand. "I've got a blue-blooded Appaloosa filly on her way here from Florida, so I need to be extra watchful."

Sam had started opening the car door when she realized Slocum was watching her. It made her cold, as if she were being watched by a snake.

"If a wild horse trespasses on my property, especially if he's trying to steal my mares, I'll get him declared a nuisance. You're a smart girl, Samantha. You know what that is. A troublemaker." He watched Sam, but she stayed frozen. "Once that's done, BLM has to catch him."

Sam's mouth was so dry she could barely pronounce the words. "And relocate him."

Slocum chuckled.

"You might want to check your facts, little lady. BLM's short of funds just now. They can't be relocating nuisance animals or keeping them locked up and eating at government expense.

"BLM *can* send that horse out of state for adoption, but that's pretty pricey, too. No, when an animal's already proven unmanageable, there's only one financially sound solution. BLM can spend a nickel on a bullet and put that stallion down."

Chapter Four ৯০

IT WAS NEARLY four o'clock when Gram's car bumped back across the River Bend bridge and Sam heard her horse calling for their afternoon ride.

Ace's sorrowful neigh turned to joyous snorting as Sam climbed out of Gram's car. No matter how full the days were on the ranch, Dad made sure Sam had time to ride.

After two years in the city, Sam had to admit her horsemanship needed polish. Dad agreed, but he assured Sam her skills would come back with practice. If he noticed she was still a little nervous since the accident, he didn't say a word.

Sam ran to her room and piled her purchases on her bed. She changed into riding clothes and nearly reached the door before Gram caught her.

"Sam, I know you're in a hurry, but please check for eggs, first. They were downright sparse this morning." Gram handed Sam a basket. "Wyatt's been craving a yellow cake with brown-sugar frosting. With him so worried over stock prices, it's the least I can do."

Sam took the egg basket and hurried to the door. She'd already fed the hens and checked their nests this morning, but fresh cake meant the delay was for a good cause.

"Oh, and as long as you're going," Gram said, pulling a tin colander from a shelf, "pick us some sugar snap peas."

Sam didn't growl aloud, but she wished she could. As the screen door slammed behind her, Ace's nicker carried over the quiet ranch.

She smooched in his direction and called, "Soon, boy."

River Bend's garden provided enough food to last all winter long, with few trips to the grocery store in Darton. As summer tapered into fall harvest, Sam couldn't go more than two hours without fetching and carrying baskets and colanders full of produce for Gram.

It took forever. The cowboys had already ridden in, giving her tired waves, by the time Sam presented Gram with sugar snap peas and eggs.

Sam jogged by the pasture on her way to the tack room. Ace had given up on her. He'd fallen to grazing again and didn't even look up.

Inside the barn, Sam heard the radio before she got to the tack room. It wasn't playing music. She heard the rustle of newspaper pages and when she walked in, Sam could see Dad wasn't reading the comics. Dad looked up to smile, but his index finger tapped his lips, hushing her. As the radio station from Reno gave the latest stock prices, he frowned.

"Hey, girl," he said, snapping the radio off. He pushed the newspaper aside, too, and rolled his shirt-sleeves down to cover red scratches on his forearms. "Back from town?"

"Yep," Sam said. She took her saddle blanket from its perch and flung Ace's bridle over her shoulder. "What did you do to your arms, Dad?"

He shrugged. "Fool bull calf got himself stuck in the blackberries, down on the other side of the river."

"Ouch," Sam said.

"Range cattle have no sense once we bring them to summer pasture," Dad mused. "They know how to find water and graze, how to kick cougars and coyotes, but give 'em something simple as a hedge full of stickers, and they only see the sweet berries. One calf—Pepper calls him Baby Huey—just won't learn. His little pink nose is *all* cut up."

Sam made a humming sound as she backed out the door balancing her saddle. She hoped it sounded like an interested hum, but not too interested. The sun showed a copper edge above the hills, hinting she should have been loping away by now.

"But Baby Huey won't be our problem for long," Dad said, turning back to his newspaper.

As if they'd suddenly frozen, Sam's hands clamped on the saddle. If Baby Huey, a spring calf, was old enough to be sold for beef, so was Buddy.

"He won't be going to market, right?" Sam asked.

Dad gave an impatient shake of his head. "Bull calf auction," he said.

Gram, or even Jake, might have picked up on Sam's hint, but Dad didn't. Instead, he came up with another chore.

"As long as you're riding out, check for Baby Huey. Then, I'm counting on you to put Ace and Sweetheart—"

"I remember," Sam interrupted, even though she'd almost forgotten. "But how do I recognize Baby Huey?"

Dad stared at Sam as if she'd asked how to tell a horse from a handsaw.

"He's bigger than the other calves, but, for crying out loud, Sam, if you see *any* calves tangled in the blackberry bushes," Dad snapped, "yank 'em out!"

"Yes, sir."

Oh, the joys of country living, Sam grumbled to herself. At Aunt Sue's house in San Francisco, she'd only had to make her bed and set the table. On a cleaning day, she might have had to dust the piano and feed the goldfish, too.

Ace's nicker made Sam look up. Her bay gelding had braved the teeth and heels of other horses to sidle toward the gate. Before she could open it, he nuzzled her neck, tickling her with whiskers and his grass-sweet breath.

"And *that*," Sam said, kissing a muzzle so dainty it could sip from a teacup, "is why I don't live in San Francisco."

Once astride Ace, Sam felt free.

She kept her reins taut. Though Ace was a cow pony, used to working on loose reins, he felt tight beneath her. Sam had learned her lesson. When Ace felt restless and ready to run, she didn't dare let her mind wander. Bucking was Ace's favorite way to make her pay attention to him.

After they'd crossed the bridge and headed north, she would let him run. When he'd settled down, they would check the blackberry bushes for cattle.

Finally, Sam leaned forward, firmed her legs, and gave Ace's ribs a tap of her heels. Even though she'd braced for Ace's sudden lunge forward, Sam grabbed the saddle horn.

No! Darn it. She only scolded herself for a second. Then, as Ace settled into a smooth run, she relaxed, swaying in the saddle as if she'd been born to it. Which she had.

His pace lulled her. Sam breathed a summer wind scented with pine, sun-yellowed grass, and an edge of evening cold. The ground underfoot slanted down into a damp hollow thick with coarse grass. A few yellow flowers no bigger than raindrops clustered together. She'd bet an underground spring ran just under the surface here.

Wings fluttered and a sage hen burst from the grass, right beneath Ace's nose. Hands steady on the reins, Sam didn't panic. *I trust you, Ace.* Her thought matched the quick stutter step that interrupted Ace's run. As Sam caught her breath, Ace swung back into a gallop. Head level, he watched the cattle that were now about a block away.

Sam slowed Ace to a jog, then a walk, and finally reined him to a stop. As Sam praised Ace by rubbing his neck, a group of white-faced Hereford calves wearing the River Bend brand sighted them. They ran bawling, brown tails straight up, to their mothers.

They were only pretending to be afraid. The calves bumped each other, detoured around a rock, then kicked their heels skyward. The calves had been around riders for weeks. They weren't a bit scared. They were playing.

Buddy would love to romp with these calves, but their fun might not last long. Some bull calves would be sold as soon as Dad found a buyer paying top price. This time next year, all the males would be on their way to market. Sam watched the calves scatter and rejoin a herd of about thirty cows.

Buddy wasn't unhappy at the ranch. Sam served as her mama, although now that she usually munched grass instead of taking a bottle, mothering mostly meant rubbing Buddy's bony head. Buddy didn't lack for playmates, either. She chased Blaze, the ranch dog, with the same zigzag silliness these calves were showing.

Eyes on the vanishing sun, Sam hurried to the hedges. She dismounted, ground-tied Ace, and checked each tangle of blackberry bushes. No sign of Baby Huey.

Angling her hand around the wicked thorns, Sam plucked one fat blue-black berry and popped it in her mouth. Oh, wow. Sam grabbed another one, closed her eyes and let the sweet juice fill her mouth. No wonder Baby Huey had been trapped so often.

Sam had caught up her reins and started to mount when she spotted another possible hiding place.

Ace hung back at the end of his reins as Sam peered into a cavelike opening in the hedges. No calf hid inside, but one might have fit. She couldn't go in, but—

All at once, Sam felt as if an icy finger had trailed down the nape of her neck. Shivering, she looked over her shoulder.

No one was there, but someone was watching. Could it be Slocum? Not likely. And she'd seen all the cowhands ride in before she'd left the ranch. And neither Gram nor Dad would come after her. They knew she'd be home in time for dinner.

Sam shrugged her shoulders so high, they nearly reached her ears. She felt cold. She studied Ace, but his eyes only scanned the terrain, showing no margin of white around the brown. He wasn't frightened, then, but Ace wasn't the most reliable watchdog. Sam wished she'd brought Blaze along.

Sam felt better once she remounted. She thought of the roast beef sandwiches, homemade french fries, and fresh steamed peas Gram was making. And the cake.

She also remembered she had to swap Sweetheart and Ace into the small corral and turn Buddy in with the horses. That could take a while, especially since she needed to be sure everyone got along. If they didn't, more than feelings could get hurt.

Sam urged Ace into a trot toward home. A rider was less vulnerable than a pedestrian. Afoot, she wasn't very fast. On Ace, she'd be tough to catch.

If she hadn't been watching for the flowers, Sam might have missed the print. The flowers were a yellow smear, and the hoofmark, distorted by the mud, looked huge.

Ace veered around the place and his pace stiffened. Sam knew a stallion had been watching her. Had it been the Phantom or the blue roan?

Gram wakened Sam early.

"Get up, sleepyhead," Gram said. "Berries are sweeter if you pick before the sun warms them."

In the dark, Sam gathered eggs and filled water troughs for the horses and hens.

In the barn corral, Ace and Sweetheart stood side by side, calm shadows against the graying sky. They looked like friends. Using her cold fingers more than her eyes, she inspected Ace for new wounds. She found none. As they'd hoped, the two horses were getting along just fine.

Filled with relief, she forked hay to Sweetheart and Ace, then scattered the grainy feed called chick-scratch for the hens.

The hens were making cautious, questioning clucks as Jake rode into the yard.

Witch, Jake's explosive black mare, looked like a dragon as she snorted hot breath into the chilly morning. Her roached mane stood up in a crest. Witch stood still as Jake dismounted. She fidgeted, though, as he tied her, not ready to stop, even though they'd loped at least five miles from Jake's ranch.

Jake gave Witch a pat, then turned toward Sam.

"What a terrifyin' sight," Jake said, bumping his Stetson back and blinking as if he couldn't believe his eyes. "Samantha Anne Forster doing work before sunup."

"I did it on the cattle drive every day," Sam reminded him as they walked toward the kitchen. Side by side, she tried to match his steps. "I've been storing up sleep for school and—"

"Biologically speaking, I don't think you can store sleep," Jake said.

If she hadn't been carrying a delicate cargo of eggs, Sam would've elbowed Jake. All her life he'd pretended to know more about everything than she did.

"Besides," Sam told him, "sleeping until seven as I usually do isn't exactly a life of luxury."

Jake gave a skeptical grunt. He opened the kitchen door, nodded her through ahead of him, and took off his hat before entering.

Gram looked up from washing dishes and frowned at the paltry number of eggs. Dad gave Sam and Jake a considering look before setting down his coffee cup.

"Jake, I want you to take the morning off from working horses," Dad said.

Jake's jaw dropped. Then he looked wary. No other chore came close to working horses. Jake believed he had the best job ever awarded to a teenager.

"Unless you have an objection?" Dad said.

Sam saw Jake's chest expand, as if he wanted to spout off a dozen objections, but he said, "No, sir."

"Go pick some berries with Sam," Dad encouraged him. "Work'll wait and maybe Grace will convince you to stay for some of her cobbler."

"I'll do better than that," Gram interrupted. "Leave Witch to spend the night and I'll drive you home with a couple pies. With school starting and her classes to prepare for, your mom sure won't have time to bake."

"So, if Gram's going to please your mom and your stomach," Sam said, "how can you say no?"

"Never planned to," Jake muttered.

Gram didn't give Jake time to change his mind. She handed them long baskets. "Fix these into the panniers on one of the pack saddles."

Sam felt that too-familiar uneasiness of not quite remembering something everyone assumed she knew. What were panniers and were the pack saddles in the tack room with all the other horse equipment?

From the corner of her eye, she saw Jake nod. Reassured, Sam kept listening as Gram rattled off instructions.

"Don't get greedy," she said. "Pick as many berries as you can, but if they're green, leave them. Indian summer usually gives us a second harvest."

"Take Banjo," Dad said. "Work some of the orneriness out of him."

In minutes, Jake had the pack saddle cinched onto Dad's big stocky bay. Dad didn't believe in coddling his favorites. If Banjo had enough energy to bully Ace, he could use it trudging along at the end of a rope, carrying berries on his back.

Sam smiled and held Banjo's head as Jake settled the baskets into side pockets on the pack saddle.

"I like you fine," she said to the Quarter horse. "But maybe you'll think twice next time about beating up on Ace."

"Let's go," Jake said. And they did.

On the way out, Sam echoed Jake's silence. They crossed the River Bend bridge, and all the time they walked, Sam watched the Calico Mountains for a flicker of silver. At first the mountains were ink blue against the sky, but as the sun rose, their peaks glowed yellow, then gold.

The cattle had moved further down the river. Though a few lifted their heads to watch the humans, most took little notice. Humans on foot weren't a threat to their serene grazing.

By the time the mountaintops turned the color of orange marmalade, they'd reached the berry bushes. There'd been no sign of the Phantom.

They worked in silence for a while, eating berries as they picked. Sweet and tart at the same time, the berries tasted like summer. The thought made Sam think about school.

"Who am I going to hang around with?"

"What's that?" Jake blinked at her, as if she'd awakened him.

"At school," Sam explained. "According to Gram, all the girls I was friends with are gone."

"The Greens sold out and moved to Oregon before they went completely broke," Jake agreed. "Linda Dennis's folks took jobs up at Lake Tahoe, running a fancy riding stable. And the Potters?" Jake shook his head. "Their spread near Darton's been subdivided for houses. Six per acre. It went for near a million dollars, I heard, so they could be living anywhere they want."

Sam felt a pulse of loyalty for her elementary

school friends. "You can't blame them. This is a hard way to make a living."

"No kidding?" Jake's voice oozed sarcasm, then he yelped. "Ow!"

She was tempted to tell Jake he'd gotten what he deserved. Pricking himself on a thorn after acting like such a big shot seemed like justice.

"So, I guess you can't answer my question." Sam slipped another handful of berries into the basket. When an especially juicy one stuck to her palm, she ate it.

"How would I know who you'd hang around with, Brat?" Jake sucked the finger he'd stabbed.

Sam fanned her face. The sun was well up now, but she didn't take off her sweatshirt because she didn't want long scratches like the ones she'd seen on Dad yesterday.

She was fanning her collar to cool herself when Jake finally ventured an opinion.

"I don't see you with Rachel Slocum's crowd," he said.

"Linc Slocum's daughter? You've got that right."

"She's cute, really popular, and she dresses like girls on TV." Jake listed those traits as if Sam might be swayed by them.

"So? With her dad, I can't think she'd be very nice. I know that's not fair, but —"

"She's nice to the right sort of people, and I doubt you'd qualify. Darrell calls her the ice queen."

Sam paused in her picking. *I doubt you'd qualify.* She shouldn't let that remark bother her, but it did. She'd spent two years away at school in San Francisco. Wouldn't that impress the queen of Smalltown, Nevada?

Then the rest of Jake's sentence sunk in.

"Isn't Darrell the one who taught you how to disable the engine of Gram's car?" Sam asked.

She recalled Jake's head under the hood of the old Buick. Jake had pulled something loose, so the car wouldn't run. It had blocked the road and she'd beaten Slocum to the Willow Springs wild horse corrals.

Jake frowned. "Since you've got such a great memory, you should remember I told you Darrell isn't a guy you need to know."

"So, why is he your friend?"

"That's different," Jake said. "You just worry about what you're going to wear and how you're going to remember your locker combination. Freshmen are always late to class because they're out crying by their lockers, trying to get their books."

Sam pictured herself in a long, empty hall. Since she'd never been good with numbers, she'd have to write the combination on her hand until she memorized it. She'd be all alone, too.

With the baskets nearly full, they'd started toward River Bend when Jake said, "Hey, you could hang around with Jen Kenworthy. Remember her?

Light hair, glasses, really smart?"

"Sure," Sam said, "but I thought she was home schooled."

"She was, for elementary school, but she started going to middle school in Darton about the time you left."

Jake's brown face took on the guilty blankness it wore when he remembered her accident and his part in it.

"I thought they owned the Gold Dust," Sam said, "but we stopped by there yesterday, and things had really changed."

"They had to sell out, and Slocum made them a good offer. He paid off their debts and kept Jen's dad on as foreman. Anyway, she'll be at the bus stop."

Just yesterday, Gram had pointed out the bus stop. She or Dad would drive Sam that far each morning, but Sam would have to walk the mile home after school.

Again, Sam's imagination went to work. She pictured herself standing there Monday morning, at sunrise, with Jen Kenworthy, a stranger.

"Jake, won't you be at the bus stop?"

Jake stopped walking. He turned toward her with the superior, tomcat smile he saved for occasions he really wanted to lord over her.

"I ride in with my brother in his Blazer."

Jake kept walking. So much for having an ally at Darton High School. Still, she couldn't give up.

"Couldn't I, maybe, ride with you? I wouldn't mind being squished."

Jake laughed, as if she'd only be able to count on his support if her life depended on it.

"No way," he said. "Freshmen take the bus."

Chapter Five ⟐

𝒯HE NAVY-BLUE horse van, pin-striped in teal, glittered like a mirage. By the way it leaned to one side, the mirage had a flat tire.

DAVISON'S HORSE TRANSPORT read the small script lettering on the door. ESTABLISHED 1975.

Dressed in business clothes and a tie, the driver stood outside the horse van, consulting a clipboard.

"Almost made it," he called out to them, smiling. "The Slocum place is only about five miles up the road, right?"

Sam and Jake glanced at each other, surprised a man with a flat tire appeared so composed.

"Right," Sam answered. "Is Mr. Slocum getting a new horse?"

She knew he was. Slocum had mentioned a blue-blooded filly on her way from Florida. Sam couldn't see inside, and the van didn't shift from side to side like a horse trailer, but she heard muffled movements within.

If the horse van's inside matched its outside, the filly probably stood in a stall lighted by a crystal chandelier. Nothing but the best for Linc Slocum.

"You betcha," the driver said. "His report on the terrain made me believe I'd be another two hours getting here. The road's a little rough but nothing like what he described. I've got time to fix this flat and still arrive early."

Jake shifted from foot to foot, eager to get on his way.

"You kids wouldn't want to walk the filly around for a few minutes, would you? She'd probably like to stretch her legs."

Banjo pulled against the lead rope and nickered toward the van. Jake didn't show the same curiosity.

"I've got to get back to work." Jake's voice fell short of being rude, but Sam knew he didn't like being called a kid.

Jake was welcome to his pride, but there was no chance Sam would turn down the opportunity to be first to see Slocum's filly.

"I'll help," Sam offered, and when Jake cleared his throat to protest, she added, "I'll see you back at the ranch, Jake."

"Whatever," he said, then gave a tug on Banjo's lead rope and walked away.

A flood of air-conditioning and an inquiring nicker accompanied the opening of the van's back doors.

Sam would bet her allowance the filly had the

bloodlines of a racing Appaloosa. From her cocoa brown head and neck to her milky body scattered with cocoa spots and barely visible striping on her hooves, the filly showed the best of her Appaloosa and Thoroughbred heritages.

On top of that, the filly's soft brown eyes, alert ears, and the way she crinkled her satiny neck to watch Sam and the driver showed she liked people.

"She's gorgeous." Sam sighed. "You're sure she belongs to Linc Slocum?"

"'Apache Hotspot,'" the driver read from his clipboard. "'Two-year-old filly by Scat Cat out of Kachina Dancer, bred at the Spanish Moss Plantation in Longview, Florida.' Bought and paid for—" He opened a door inside the van to show a mini-apartment with champagne-colored carpet and tiled walls. "And I do mean *paid* for!"

"What's that?" Sam pointed inside the van, above a clean-scrubbed feed manger. "It looks like a video camera."

"Closed-circuit TV," the driver said, nodding. "I have a screen up front, so I can see what she's doing at any moment during our drive."

"Wow," Sam said.

With ease, the driver backed the Appaloosa from the van and handed her lead rope to Sam.

"Be out in a minute," he said, ducking toward the mini-apartment. "Gonna put on a coverall, to change that tire."

The Appaloosa was tall. Nearly sixteen hands, Sam guessed, and she moved with a spirited strength that made Sam keep both hands on the lead rope.

The Appaloosa scanned the open terrain and trembled. She stared at the flat, sage-dotted range, at the red-winged blackbirds balancing on tall grass, at the oatmeal colored hills clumped along the horizon. Clearly, Hotspot wasn't used to open spaces. Head held high, she neighed after Banjo.

Her neigh was like music. Heading home, Jake fought to keep Banjo moving in the opposite direction. As the filly neighed again, Sam knew she'd never heard anything like the melodious sound. Any horse within hearing distance would yearn to investigate.

Sam could hear the clink of metal tools as the driver worked on the tire and hummed.

Hotspot skittered in an arc, trying to scan all the hills at once. The effect was like a dog winding its leash around its walker. Was the driver watching? Sam backed away from the horse, trying to guide the filly as if she were on a longe line.

"Hey, girl," Sam said. "You're fine."

She couldn't let the horse hurt herself. Wrapped for travel, Hotspot's slim legs looked even more delicate.

Sam was about to call the van driver and turn responsibility for the costly filly back to him, when Hotspot stopped. She flung her head so high, Sam stood on tiptoe to grip the rope beneath the filly's chin. Her nostrils quivered with a sweet nicker.

Sam didn't have the Appaloosa's acute sense of smell nor the fine hearing that keeps horses ahead of predators, but she could feel the morning grow still around her.

Small stones rattled down the hillside. Sam stared until her eyes burned, knowing what she'd see if she was patient. At last, he appeared.

The Phantom didn't move. Like a statue carved of silver-flecked marble, he stood camouflaged against a granite boulder.

Hotspot gave a worried nicker. The filly from Florida had never seen a wild stallion. Her muscles bunched to run.

Sam wrapped the lead more tightly around her hand. If Hotspot bolted, Sam could use only her body as an anchor. Even that might be hopeless, since Sam couldn't tell if Hotspot was frightened or excited.

Still motionless, the Phantom studied the van, filly, and Sam. Finally, he decided to prance closer. The play of muscles seemed to polish his hide from the inside. The Phantom arched his neck until his chin bumped his chest. Dark eyes peered through the forelock cascading over his face.

Show-off, Sam thought, but she didn't speak.

Since his rough capture, she'd only seen the Phantom once, when the blue roan stallion attempted to take the Phantom's mares.

Would Sam see the Phantom only when other

horses acted as bait?

Oh no! Sam's attention had wandered and the filly bolted. Sam settled into a crouch, keeping her weight low as the horse spun around her.

"What's up?" The driver slid from beneath the van, still holding a wrench.

"I—" Sam kept her back to the hillside. *Don't look behind me. There's no beautiful wild stallion, there.*

Sam swallowed, as the filly slowed.

Don't look, she thought. How could she explain Hotspot's excitement without pointing out the Phantom?

She must think of something. If the driver saw the silver stallion, he'd surely mention him to Slocum. That would convince Slocum that the Phantom had slipped in and tried to steal Kitty.

Slocum was already worried that a renegade stallion would seek out his blue bloods. Tales of this encounter would only increase his worry.

Sam resisted the urge to look back over her shoulder. She kept her eyes on the driver. His frown faded as the filly calmed down. Sam did what she could to draw the rest of his attention.

"Wow!" Sam brushed dirt from her jeans. "I think all this open space scared her." She stroked Hotspot's satiny neck. "Do you think that's possible?"

The filly sneezed at the dust she'd stirred, then struck out with one foreleg.

"Could be." The driver walked closer, and Hotspot

extended her muzzle for rubbing.

"She seems fine, now," Sam said.

Then, since the driver's attention was fixed on the filly, Sam sneaked a look at the hillside. Rocks. Dirt. Sagebrush. No Phantom.

A breath sighed through Sam's lips as she returned her attention to the Appaloosa. Again, she thought how suited this driver was to his job.

He let the filly lip his empty hand. He didn't seem to mind that she smeared him with horse spit.

"You're just a pet, aren't you?" He asked the horse. "I hope this Slocum knows how to treat a lady like you."

Pictures of bloody spurs, cruel bits, and the Phantom's scar flashed through Sam's mind. What she hoped was that Slocum hadn't purchased this sweet filly for himself.

A thunderstorm ruined the last day of summer vacation.

Dad roused Sam early to ride out with the hands. He needed another pair of eyes to spot and chase all the cattle out of the canyons and draws. During droughts, storms like this could cause flash floods. Sudden rains filled low spots, overflowed them, then followed long valleys. When the water crested it created furious rivers. Each year, cattle drowned. They were safer on the flats, near the ranch. This year River Bend couldn't afford to lose even one.

In spite of the rolling booms of thunder, the rain was only a light sprinkle. The cattle stayed together and the job went fast. By eight o'clock in the morning, Sam stood on River Bend's front porch, peeling off her yellow slicker.

This time tomorrow, she'd be walking into her first high school class. Sam hung her slicker on a hook and wondered if she'd like Darton High.

She slicked back her damp hair and wished she could shake dry like Blaze.

Sam noticed Gram standing near the counter, regarding the half-full egg basket.

"Thanks for taking care of the chickens, Gram," she said.

"You're welcome, but I'll tell you, Samantha, something's wrong. Six eggs for fourteen hens is just not normal." Gram shook her head and scooped a serving of warm blackberry cobbler from a square ceramic pan.

"Oh, yum." Sam watched Gram drizzle fresh cream over the top. Sam took the bowl of cobbler, even though she'd eaten so much pie last night that she'd vowed not to touch another blackberry until next summer.

"Have you seen any tracks around the chicken coop?" Gram asked. "Skunk or raccoon tracks? Blaze would wake us if a coyote was getting in."

Sam didn't admit she hadn't thought to search out tracks. "Maybe the hens are sick," she said. "Or getting old."

Sam hesitated to make such suggestions, since Dad insisted every creature on the ranch needed to contribute.

"It's a sad fact that when chickens get sick, they usually die," Gram said. "There's rarely time to call the vet. And those are young hens. Many times, Wyatt's said he won't run a home for old chickens."

A thunderclap rattled the windows. Sam looked out to the big pasture, suddenly worried for her orphan calf. She spotted Buddy instantly. She was running, jumping, and landing in mud puddles for the sheer fun of making a splash.

Still, Sam bit her lip with worry. If Dad wouldn't run a home for old chickens, he probably wouldn't run one for pet calves. Sam half turned toward Gram, then lost her nerve. She just couldn't ask.

Just the same, Gram met her eyes.

"No way you can put it off any longer," Gram said.

Sam's heart vaulted up. The final bit of cobbler wobbled on the spoon, then fell back into the bowl with a plop.

"This mess" — Gram gestured toward rain rivulets on the windows — "probably won't let up until late afternoon, and then you'll want to ride. You'd better get upstairs and try on those clothes from Aunt Sue."

Gram couldn't have picked a more effective way to get Sam moving. For one horribly long second, she'd thought Gram wanted to discuss Buddy's future as a beefsteak.

"Yep, you're right," Sam said, rinsing her bowl at the sink. "I'll get up there and try on every single thing."

"Call me if you need help making any decisions," Gram called after her, but Sam was fleet with relief, and barely heard.

At the end of an hour, Sam had no doubt she'd grown since coming home. All her jeans were too short. In fact, only one pair of pants fit.

Sam frowned at the gray cords she couldn't remember choosing. She guessed she'd have to learn to like them.

Most of her blouses were snug in the shoulders, maybe because she'd developed muscles lifting hay bales, carrying saddles, and juggling her squirming calf.

She had an almost-new, hippie-style skirt she'd bought in San Francisco, but she couldn't imagine wearing it to school in Darton.

Sam stood in front of the mirror on the back of her bedroom door. The skirt was crinkly and dark green. Maybe she could wear it for a holiday party, but she couldn't remember anything more festive than going to Christmas Eve service at the Methodist church in Darton.

Sam gave the mirror a more intent look. She liked her slightly wider shoulders, new height, and general fitness. She was glad her waist curved in and she had a chest that was *there* but not to an embarrassing extent.

She hated her hair. Sam leaned close to the mirror

and made a face. Instead of making her look older, it made her look ready for Halloween.

That hair would ruin her first day of school, no matter what she wore.

Unless . . .

Sam took a strand of damp hair and pulled it straight. It reached just below her cheekbone. Gram probably wouldn't approve. Jake's reaction didn't bear imagining. Dad, on the other hand, might not holler if she cut it again.

Sam held her breath and squinted her eyes at the mirror. A new start and a new look.

Gram had said to call if she had trouble making any decisions, but Sam didn't. She walked downstairs, pretending she had a short, boyish cut.

Maybe, she thought with each step. Just maybe.

By the time she reached the kitchen, Sam had made up her mind. The announcement burst from her lips, almost without her permission, "I hate this weird hair and I'm chopping it off!"

"All right, dear," Gram said. She sat at the kitchen table, across from a younger woman with a long red braid. "But first you might say hello to our guest. You remember Miss Olson from the BLM, don't you? She's come to talk with you about that mustang you call the Phantom."

Chapter Six ❧

ℬRYNNA OLSON, director of the Willow Springs Wild Horse Center, wore a crisply pressed khaki uniform and a name tag. Her red hair was confined in a no-nonsense French braid. The only thing interfering with her professional appearance was the big bowl of blackberry cobbler centered before her.

"Hi, Samantha." Miss Olson's tone was warm but only for an instant. "Your grandmother says you've heard Mr. Slocum's concerns about a mustang stallion trespassing on his property and stealing his mares."

Miss Olson's expression didn't betray her feelings about the accusation, but Sam could guess what they were. After the Phantom's capture, Miss Olson had watched the stallion's untamed fury with the understanding of a horsewoman.

"There's no way it was the Phantom." Sam defended her horse by reflex. "What does Slocum—"

Sam shook her head as Gram cleared her throat " —*Mr.* Slocum expect you to do?"

"I'm holding him off for now, but he wants action." Miss Olson pushed her bowl aside, as if she'd lost her appetite. "Since I disqualified his application to adopt a wild horse, Mr. Slocum is unhappy. He doesn't care for me and doesn't respect my position with the federal government."

Sam stared out the kitchen window, but she didn't say what she was thinking.

Outside, rain dripped from the eaves of the white ranch house. Sam knew many ranchers distrusted the BLM. Ranch families were independent minded. They didn't like government rules telling them how to live on land they'd ranched for generations.

Slocum despised the BLM for a different reason than most.

The rain increased, but it fell so slowly, Sam could almost count the drops. The sky was blue-gray, still deciding whether the storm had ended.

When Sam turned back to Miss Olson, the BLM official's half smile said she didn't expect Gram or Sam to defend her or the government agency. Besides, Sam was pretty sure Miss Olson could stand up for herself.

"Respect me or not, Mr. Slocum wants the BLM to catch the wild horse he feels is stalking his mares."

"Are you going to do it?" Sam asked.

"We're not convinced there is a renegade stallion,"

Miss Olson said. "The teeth slashes on his mare could have come from any horse.

"He said she'd been wandering the range. Folks aren't supposed to turn domestic stock out, but they do. Some escape or are stolen, too." Miss Olson turned to Gram. "I had an e-mail this morning from one of our California offices. A valuable stallion is missing and presumed stolen. His owner's frantic, hoping he's on the loose."

"Horse thieves even in these modern times," Gram said, shaking her head.

Sam wished she could tell the stallion's owner not to give up. After all, everyone had believed Blackie was gone for good.

"More than likely"—Miss Olson's tone sharpened—"the sorrel was bitten by one of Slocum's own horses."

Sam nodded and kept her lips pressed together.

"Before we waste manpower setting a trap for a trespassing stallion that may not exist, Mr. Slocum has to give us some evidence he's right."

"Like tracks?" Sam asked.

"That would be a start," Miss Olson said, "but there's no shortage of unshod horses around here."

Gram took a sip of her coffee, then frowned. Sam could see Gram was so intent on listening, she'd let her coffee grow cold.

"From what you've seen of the Phantom"—Miss Olson watched Sam with such intensity, Sam wanted to say no to whatever she asked—"would he enter an enclosed area like Slocum's ranch?"

Sam stared at the tabletop. She pictured the remote-controlled iron gates, the grassy approach to the pens, ranch house, and mansion.

Up until today, Sam would have sworn Phantom wouldn't enter such an area. But after he'd materialized out of nowhere to eye Hotspot, could she be sure?

"He's never crossed the river," Sam said. "The closest he's come is halfway."

Chills covered Sam's arms as she thought of the beautiful stallion, silvered with moonlight, as he swam out to her. The Phantom remembered he'd once been her colt and he remembered his secret name.

Sam sighed. Though Miss Olson took the sound as sadness, she didn't turn all sensitive and gooey. She merely agreed.

"Based on what I saw when he was in captivity, that stallion wouldn't willingly enter any fenced area. He showed more resistance to confinement than I've witnessed in any mustang."

"What will you do if Mr. Slocum comes up with some sort of evidence?" Gram asked.

Miss Olson looked thoughtful. She didn't seem to notice she'd pressed her palms together and matched her fingers as she tapped them against her lips.

"We're shorthanded because we lost Flick."

The glance Miss Olson shot Sam asked if she

remembered the cowboy who'd used his position with the BLM to capture the Phantom for Slocum. Sam nodded.

"And the college kids who were working for us are on their way back to school." Miss Olson turned in her chair to watch the weather outside the window. "I should get back," she said, standing, but her expression said she'd rather stay in Gram's warm kitchen.

"Frankly, it's hard to find people with the expertise to track and capture horses." Miss Olson raised one eyebrow as she looked at Gram.

"I wish I could help," Gram said, "but the only folks I know who are good at that sort of thing are Jake and Wyatt."

Miss Olson looked sheepish, but she said, "It pays a lot more than you'd think."

Gram made a considering sound, but Sam didn't know why. Dad wouldn't take a job with the BLM unless he was in danger of losing the ranch.

Money. Why did every conversation lead back to money?

Sam smoothed her hands over her hair. Even if Gram agreed to drive her into Darton to get her hair cut, it would cost something. If the Forster family couldn't afford an extra pair of jeans, they couldn't pay a stylist to snip her hair into a fashionable shape.

Sam was sure Gram had already forgotten her outburst as she'd come pounding downstairs.

Apparently, Miss Olson hadn't.

With her hand on the doorknob, Miss Olson stopped. She turned so quickly, her braid snapped from one side of her neck to the other.

"Well, shoot," she said. "It's too late to go back to Willow Springs now. Samantha, I might be able to help you out. When I was going to college, I was the dorm queen at cutting hair. If your grandmother doesn't mind, I'd be glad to—" she searched for the right word "—even things up a little."

"Miss Olson, that would be awfully nice of you," Gram said. "And you'll just have to stay for dinner."

"I'd love to, if I didn't have so many hungry animals waiting at home," Miss Olson said. "But if Sam grabs a pair of sharp scissors and leads me to a mirror, I'll see what I can do."

By the time she'd dampened, combed, and snipped at Sam's hair, Miss Olson's voice had turned less formal.

"This is embarrassing to mention, but I liked it better a couple weeks ago when you called me Brynna."

Sam's brown eyes tried to catch the redhead's blue ones in the mirror, but they only darted away.

"Okay," Sam said.

Brynna worked along Sam's neck for a minute before she spoke again. "And since you're tuned in to the way wild horses think, I'd like your opinion of what's going on with Slocum's mare."

Sam thought of the aggressive blue roan. She thought of the Phantom coming to see Hotspot. It wasn't safe to mention either.

This time, Brynna did meet Sam's eyes in the mirror. "Please, I'd like to get this cleared up as soon as possible," she said. "If it's a secret, I'll take it to my grave."

Brynna looked sincere. Sam could explain how the blue roan had swum the river, waded ashore, and trotted right up to the corral fence, but stubborness kept her quiet.

Brynna seemed nice enough, but Sam couldn't shake off years of hearing that the BLM rarely worked in the best interests of ranchers.

And yet Brynna had kept the Phantom free.

A knot of confusion tightened in Sam's stomach. Maybe she should talk with Jake.

"Have you heard unexplained sounds, especially at night? Any sign of an intruder?"

"Gram thinks a skunk might be getting in the chicken coop," Sam offered.

Brynna grumbled, but she kept combing and cutting. At last, Sam decided she could tell half the truth. After all, she'd been with Gram when the blue roan challenged the Phantom.

"On the way back from Darton, we saw the Phantom," Sam said.

"You did? Where was that?" Brynna stayed calm,

but Sam could tell she was hoping for a revelation.

"Near War Drum Flats," Sam said. She'd bet Brynna was calculating how close that was to Slocum's ranch. "He was running off a bachelor stallion trying to steal some of his mares."

"Nothing unusual about that." Brynna sounded disappointed.

"He's a blue roan."

Brynna shrugged. "I'll keep an eye out for him, but—"

"About fourteen hands, with a hammer head," Sam said, but Brynna didn't take the hint.

"We're looking for a mustang that doesn't fear human habitation. That points to your colt."

Sam stared blindly into the mirror, until Brynna touched her shoulder and asked, "So, what do you think of your hair?"

Sam studied her reflection. Her red-brown hair lay in neat, glossy wisps around her face, and her bangs were layered so they poufed up just a little.

It was a plain haircut that didn't draw attention to itself, but it did make her eyes look bigger.

"Thanks, Brynna." Sam touched the tendrils that curved against her neck. "It looks great."

"That's an exaggeration," Brynna said, heading toward the stairs, "but thanks."

Sam walked Brynna downstairs and past Gram, who still wanted her to stay for dinner.

Sam grabbed her slicker and followed Brynna

through the kitchen door. Outside, a fine rain came down, making a hissing sound. Tiny raindrops hit the dirt and bounced up like powdered sugar.

They were halfway to the white government truck when the woman shooed her off.

"Go on back," Brynna said. "And have a good first day at school."

"I will!" Sam shouted over another clap of thunder.

She'd started back to the house, when movement drew her attention to the barn.

Light shone golden and cozy from the open barn. Dad stood in the doorway. Dad's dark silhouette showed one hand planted against the doorway. The other hung loose as he looked through the curtains of misty rain.

Was Dad angry because they'd invited the BLM official in from the storm? Did he suspect Sam was engineering a secret wild horse adoption? Was he too tired to make a polite trip across the yard to say hello?

Sam quit guessing. She must be mistaken, because from here, it looked like Dad was staring after Brynna with something like a smile.

Sam's alarm was set. Her clothes hung on her closet door. A backpack stuffed with notebooks, pencils and pens, and a tiny tub of lip gloss sat by her bedroom door. Everything was ready for her first day of school, and still she felt restless, as if she'd left something important undone.

Sam stared at her ceiling. Twice, it turned pale, brightened by faraway glimmers of lightning.

The house stood so silent, it was creepy. Sam held her breath, listening. She heard the kitchen clock. A floorboard squeaked. That would be Blaze, chasing dream cats while he slept in front of the empty fireplace.

The only sounds came from outside. The rain had stopped, but thunder grumbled in the clouds. Sam couldn't tell if the storm was moving away or coming back.

She hoped it had gone, because it was one more thing Dad worried about.

After she'd gone to bed, Sam had overheard Dad talking with Gram about hay. Dad always counted on a September harvest. Now, because of the rain, he was afraid he wouldn't get it. So far the rain had been light, but he didn't want to risk a long wet spell. Wet hay could rot. If it did, they couldn't afford to buy good hay from someone else.

She'd heard him slap his palm against the table.

"A single hundred-degree day is all I need. We could cut and dry that entire field of alfalfa one day and bale it the next."

The numbers on Sam's watch glowed blue-green in the darkness. Midnight. This was the time the Phantom had come to the river.

He hadn't come since his capture, and she had no

reason to believe he would come tonight. He couldn't know tomorrow was special to her. Even if he did, what would a first day of school mean to a horse?

The thunder boomed. Closer. *Rain, rain, go away. Come again another day.* The nursery rhyme meant something to a rancher's daughter.

Blaze's toenails clicked across the kitchen floor, then Sam heard him drink from his water bowl. By the sound of his lapping, he didn't have much left.

Grabbing at the excuse, Sam swung her legs out from under the covers. Quickly and quietly, she moved through the dark house to the kitchen and refilled Blaze's water bowl.

With the dog's noisy drinking to cover her movements, Sam opened the door and slipped outside.

Mud-scented wind blew Sam's nightgown behind her, but nothing else moved. Holding to a porch post, she leaned out as far as she could, staring toward the river.

Starlight showed the sway of a few trees. If the clouds blew aside, unveiling the moon, she might see the Phantom standing on the other side of the river.

Of course, that idea made no sense. When even night birds were tucked into dry nests, why would the stallion be out?

A crack, a sizzle, a glare of white-gold light ripped a crooked path across the black sky. Sam caught her breath and smelled a metallic heat at the moment she saw him.

The Phantom reared on the other side of the river. Like a frosty tree turned upside down, branches of lightning ran jagged behind the stallion.

The Phantom had come back!

Sam's arms clamped around herself. She was scared, excited, and she had no choice. The stallion had returned. She couldn't leave him rearing alone in the darkness.

Sam had lifted the hem of her nightgown and her toes had pressed into the squishy mud, when the porch light flashed on. For an instant, she imagined it was more lightning, but Dad's solemn voice left her no escape from the truth.

"Samantha, get back inside."

"But, Dad—"

"No excuses. We'll talk about this tomorrow."

She'd been caught. She'd be grounded. Worst of all, the Phantom would go on waiting in the darkness, thinking she'd forgotten.

Chapter Seven ❧

Sam was already sitting on her neatly made bed, dressed and ready for school, when her alarm went off.

If she had just one friend, today would be easier. If Dad weren't angry and likely to lecture while he drove her to the bus stop, today would be easier. If she could go for a gallop on Ace after school, today would be easier. But none of that would happen.

Face it, Sam told herself as she switched off her shrilling alarm clock, today is *not* going to be easy.

Breakfast was not on the table. Nothing sizzled on the stove. Yes, she'd told Gram she only wanted cereal and toast on school days, but this felt wrong.

Dad stood at the window, staring out at the gray morning.

"Dad, I—"

"Eat some breakfast. Gram's out doing your chores."

A lump swelled in Sam's throat. Worry over last night had knocked thoughts of morning chores right out of her head. Out in the wind-tossed yard, Gram was filling water troughs, feeding Ace, finding eggs.

"I've still got time." Sam glanced at her watch. "I'll go stop her."

"She's doing it as a favor. Just for today. Now, get something to eat."

"Okay," Sam said.

Even though he wouldn't turn to look at her, Dad didn't sound too angry. Still, he wouldn't change his mind about grounding her. Dad was stubborn and so darn sure he was right.

The only question was how long she'd be grounded.

Sam poured milk on her cereal and considered Dad's stiff back. The smartest thing she could do was wait for him to explain her punishment, instead of harassing him about it.

Sam tried to be patient. She finished her cereal, managed to eat some toast, then rinsed her bowl. As Gram came back inside, Sam kissed her good-bye, climbed into the truck, and held her backpack on her lap as Dad drove toward the bus stop.

The rain-washed sky spread bright blue above the Calico Mountains, but Sam's chest felt tight. Her teeth hurt from clenching. She knew that if she didn't ask Dad about being grounded, she'd burst into tears when the first little thing went wrong.

She couldn't let that happen on her first day at the bus stop. Even if she ended up waiting there alone, she'd be examined as a newcomer as she entered that bus. How cool would it be to appear with red, swollen eyes, looking like a kindergartner afraid to leave home?

Sam took such a deep breath, Dad must have heard her question coming.

"For how long?" she asked. "How long before I can ride Ace?"

"We'll start with a week and see how it goes," Dad said.

A week. Seven days. That wasn't so long. She could stand it.

"And the fall drive? Will I be able to ride in time to help bring the cattle in?"

"No."

Seven days. Not so long, but time enough to keep her from riding Ace, her hat held down by its stampede string as the wind whistled past. Long enough for her to miss a once-a-year event.

"Since you're already mad at me," Sam began, and noticed Dad didn't correct her, "are you going to butcher Buddy?"

The truck slowed as if Dad had lifted his boot from the gas pedal.

"What in —?" He twisted toward her. "What in the *world* are you thinking, Samantha?"

"About money," she said. "I'm thinking that we need every dollar we can make from the hay and the cattle."

Dad shook off his surprise, and the truck surged forward again.

"First off, we only raise enough hay for our own stock. I don't like to buy it over the winter. Second, when we get so poor one pet calf would save us—" Dad's mouth curved up at one corner, but his expression wasn't quite a smile. "Well, let's just say I'd put you to work long before that happened."

"I'd go to work," Sam offered, "if it meant keeping Buddy. Sure I would." She pictured the mall at Darton and wondered how old you'd have to be to work in the food court. "I bet I could find a job after school. Do you want me to do it?"

Sam couldn't interpret Dad's expression. It flickered somewhere between proud and embarrassed.

"I'll let you know," he said.

The truck slowed again. The bus stop was just ahead.

Dad braked, turned toward Sam, and leaned across to touch her cheek.

"Your hair looks real cute that way, Samantha." Dad nodded three times.

Sam knew he wanted to add something else. She glanced down the road. The bus wasn't in sight, so she waited.

"Honey, there's not a darn thing wrong that time

won't fix," Dad said. "Now, you go on and have a nice first day."

Sam walked toward the girl standing at the bus stop. Uneasy because she knew the girl was watching her, too, Sam tried not to stare.

The other girl was thin. Not model trim or athlete lean, but downright gawky. She wore dark-framed glasses, and her white-blond hair hung in skinny braids. They ended in tassels that made them look like exclamation marks.

She wore a hot orange tee shirt, jeans, and black high-top tennis shoes. Showing through the mesh pocket of her backpack was the most complicated-looking calculator Sam had ever seen.

Sam gathered her courage, trying to think of something to say, but the other girl beat her to it.

"Hi. I'm Jennifer Kenworthy. If you're Samantha Forster, I think we've met before, a long time ago."

"I am," Sam said. "And I sort of remember that, too." But this wasn't the timid girl Sam recalled. "I usually go by Sam."

"Good. I go by Jen, or Jennifer, but never Jenny—except to my mom."

They both smiled, then Jen's face took on a puzzled look. "Why did Jake tell me your hair was kind of punk-looking?"

"He didn't know any better," Sam said. "It was, until last night. I had a trim and he hasn't seen it yet."

Jake didn't take change in stride. Sam thought of the morning after the Phantom had accidentally given her a black eye. When she'd tried to cover it with makeup and a bold attitude, Jake had exploded.

"That's pretty dramatic," Jen said. "All I did for the first day of school is break my poor mother's heart. Not really. That's just what she said, because I insisted on dressing like a normal kid. Last year, when I started going to public school, my mom made me wear skirts and twinsets. This year, I'm dressing myself."

About time, Sam thought. She'd been selecting her own clothes forever. But she only said, "Looks good to me."

"Thanks," Jen said. "Mom said I was dressed to go muck out stalls, but I stood firm. The thing is"—Jen lowered her voice—"I don't really care."

"So, you have horses?"

A queasy look crossed Jen's face, and Sam worried that she'd ended the friendship before it had begun. How could she have forgotten what Jake had told her? The Kenworthys had been on the verge of losing their ranch when Slocum offered to buy it.

"Well, yeah," Jen said. "You remember—"

"I do. Sorry," Sam apologized. "I forgot."

"No big deal." Jen ducked her head. "After all, *I* forgot you, uh, didn't have a mom to say stupid things to you, like mine does."

Silence simmered between them for a minute.

They'd both messed up and admitted it. That seemed a fine beginning for a friendship.

"But, yeah," Jen said at last, "we still have a few horses. Mine is Silk Stocking, but I call her Silly. She's a truly ditzy palomino mare." Jen shook her head, then added, "I plan to be a vet, though, and she's better than a textbook on horse neuroses."

"She'd probably get along great with Ace, my little mustang. All the other horses like to push him around." Sam met Jen's eyes. Clearly, they both loved their horses, no matter what. "We should go ride sometime."

The roar of the yellow school bus ended their conversation. Jen didn't do more than nod, and Sam didn't mention the ride would have to wait until she was out of trouble.

The morning hours were filled with slamming lockers, ringing bells, and shouting voices. Guided by a useless photocopied map, Sam navigated miles of mazelike halls. She made it to each class on time, but Jake's warning about weeping freshmen kept her from visiting her locker until lunch hour.

Arms aching, Sam approached her locker, carrying every book from each morning class. In little tiny ink numbers, she'd written her combination on the inside of her wrist.

Her locker opened like a dream. Sam arranged her books inside, closed it, and opened it again, this time without consulting the numbers on her wrist.

When a group of laughing girls passed by, Sam looked at her watch, pretending she had someplace to go. She didn't. She'd had English class with Jen, but Jen hadn't mentioned meeting for lunch. And Sam hadn't seen Jake.

She decided not to wander around looking lost. Instead, she pulled an apple from her backpack and wished the break would end. She practiced opening her locker again. She had journalism after lunch. She'd been on the newspaper staff in middle school, and her teacher had said she had talent. Sam was excited to give it a try in high school.

She might meet some people, too. Although a lot of the other students were strangers to each other, Sam had felt too shy to speak to people in her other classes. She hoped journalism was less formal. Maybe there she could relax and make some friends.

Sam closed her locker. She turned the dial very deliberately, in case anyone was watching.

At last, the bell rang. A stampede of students filled the halls, but it was a knot of rowdy boys she noticed. As they forged a path through the other kids, Sam saw Jake. The quietest of them all, he moved along in the center, grinning.

Until he saw Sam. Then, Jake came to such a sudden stop, another student rammed into him from behind. Jake staggered forward a step, but his eyes stayed on Sam.

Jake hated her short hair. That was clear. He kept going—without waving, without saying hi, without recognizing she was alive.

He'd get used to it, Sam told herself. It's not like she'd planned to tag along with him at school. She'd see him at home and he could spout off about the mistake she'd made.

Right now, she'd better hurry to class.

"We've got to hit the ground running," said Mr. Blair.

Sam's journalism teacher looked more like a football coach as he fired off orders. Half the students loitered near a row of computers. The other half sat at attention in desks ranged in straight rows.

The students whispering by the computers must be the veterans, Sam thought. The students who were seated and attentive, Sam admitted, looked like freshmen.

"Class time is for putting out a newspaper. The textbook is for teaching you how to write. Here's a schedule." Mr. Blair flapped a sheaf of papers. "Do two chapters each night and turn in the work every day when you get to class." Mr. Blair took a breath, then pointed. "What did I say?"

"I, uh—" said a boy wearing a black tee shirt.

"That's what I thought." Mr. Blair turned toward Sam and pointed. "What did I say?"

"We're putting out the newspaper during class

and reading the book at night." Sam rattled off what she remembered. "We turn in the work—" When Sam saw Mr. Blair's eyes narrow, she hurried to correct herself. "We turn in *two* chapters' worth of work every day."

"Okay." Mr. Blair turned toward a bespectacled boy who sat with his feet atop a big wooden desk. "RJay, give this girl a story." Mr. Blair jerked his thumb toward Sam, then asked, "Name?"

"Sam," she said, lacing her fingers together in her lap to keep her hands from shaking. Then, as Mr. Blair scanned the student list in his hand, she added, quietly, "*Samantha* Forster."

"Hmm. A freshman." Mr. Blair stared so long, Sam thought it very possible he was trying to read her mind. "Give her a story anyway, RJay."

The teacher shooed her toward RJay.

Feeling singled out, Sam crossed the room. She tugged at the hem of her scoop-neck white shirt, even though she knew it looked fine with her new jeans. Today, she'd seen a hundred girls dressed the same way, but Sam still felt awkward as she stood before RJay. She guessed he was the editor of *Dialogue*, the Darton High newspaper, but he said nothing to confirm it.

"Go see Rachel," RJay said, and then he, too, pointed.

At first, Sam didn't recognize the name.

Rachel looked like a model. Her sleek hair was

the dark brown of coffee. She wore a short, trendy plaid skirt with suspenders. On most girls, it would look silly. On her, worn over a crisp white blouse, it looked great.

Rachel let Sam stand and wait while she talked to a blonde in a cheerleader's uniform embroidered with the name *Daisy*. Gradually, Rachel turned.

Her rose-gold fingernails skimmed the wing of hair slanting across her forehead, lifting it away from her eyes. She scanned Sam from head to waist, but still said nothing.

Sam turned hot with embarrassment. She felt like such a reject, but she had to say something.

"RJay said you'd assign me a story," Sam explained.

"Back-to-school interview with Ms. Santos," Rachel ran the words together, sounding bored and faintly British.

Sam frowned. *Ms. Santos*. Her ignorance only deepened her blush.

"Where would I find her?" she asked. After she found her, maybe she'd figure out who she was.

"Oh." Rachel stretched the word so that it sounded like *ow*. Did Rachel have an English accent or was she pretending? Sam couldn't tell, but all at once she remembered. When they were out picking berries, hadn't Jake said Linc Slocum's daughter was named Rachel? Hadn't he said Slocum was divorced and that Rachel and her brother spent summers in

London with their mother?

"Oh," Rachel said again, eyes sliding toward the cheerleader. "I guess the little cowgirl"—she pronounced it *cow gull*, and studied Sam's shoes as if looking for traces of manure—"can't be expected to know Ms. Santos is our principal."

Cowgirl. Sam swallowed hard. At River Bend Ranch, she would consider that description a compliment. Here at school, from Rachel, it clearly wasn't.

On the other hand, cowgirls were tough. They stood up to trouble.

"You're right," Sam said, lifting her chin just a little. "I've been going to school in San Francisco and I don't know a lot of the local people."

"San Francisco?" asked the cheerleader.

"San Francisco isn't London, honey," Rachel said, but the snub fell short when Mr. Blair interrupted.

"Rachel's grasp of geography is quite astounding," he said. Then he glanced at the classroom clock and back at Sam. "Run over to the office and schedule that interview."

Sam grabbed her notebook, wondering what in the world she'd ask Ms. Santos if she was available.

Think fast, Sam ordered herself. She'd been on her middle school newspaper. She could do this.

So what if she didn't have time to make a list of questions or review what a "back-to-school" interview should include?

With determined steps, Sam headed toward the door.

"Don't be surprised if she puts you off until tomorrow," Mr. Blair called. "I have a feeling Ms. Santos is rather busy today, Samantha."

Sam was headed toward the door, when Rachel's silky laughter came after her.

"*Samantha*. See, Daisy, you lose. You thought she was a boy."

Chapter Eight ॐ

SAM WAVED GOOD-BYE to Jen, then started the long walk home.

Late August sun shone on the bare nape of her neck as if yesterday's storm had never happened. It didn't feel like the one-hundred-degree day Dad had wished for, but it was plenty hot.

Sam grumbled to herself. This walk ought to count as a chore. It wouldn't, of course. She'd need to check the hens' nests for eggs and make sure the animals were fed. Monday was also laundry day. Even though Gram had a perfectly good clothes dryer, she hung fresh laundry on a clothesline. She expected Sam to take it down and fold it. Sam lengthened her stride, hurrying. She had to admit that her sun-dried sheets always smelled better than those tumbled in the dryer.

Something moved.

Sam stopped. Because it could be the Phantom,

Mustang Moon **89**

she didn't turn to face the movement. Instead, she stood still, letting her eyes search until they found a rabbit crouched on his haunches, watching. It was close enough that she saw its nose twitch.

When Sam started walking again, the sand-colored rabbit launched itself across the desert in the opposite direction.

It could have been the Phantom, but it wasn't. Sam's heart sank as she remembered last night. The Phantom had come to her, rearing against a turmoil of stars and lightning, but she hadn't been able to go to him.

How unfair. Sam lengthened her stride as she grew angry. Not only was she grounded, she hadn't even done the thing she was being punished for.

There was no use talking to Dad. She could only hope the Phantom spotted her on one of these afternoon hikes home.

Thoughts of the stallion pulled at her heart.

She remembered the tickle of his whiskery muzzle as he'd nuzzled her hand when they both stood in the river. She remembered that amazing day at the Willow Springs corrals, when he'd put aside his hatred of humans to rest his great, heavy head on her shoulder.

Sam was almost home when she heard hooves and saw Buddy streaking toward her.

"What are you doing out here?" she shouted.

The calf kept coming at a clumsy run, her front

legs running to the right while her rear legs swung left. Ross, a River Bend cowboy, rode behind her at a lope.

Sam realized the big-eyed calf had no intention of stopping, so she braced her feet apart. Even though Sam was standing firm as Buddy plowed into her, the calf nearly knocked her down.

"Settle down, girl," Sam said.

Buddy curled around her, streaking Sam's new jeans with dust. The calf walked two laps before stopping and finally pressing against Sam's side to face Ross.

"Good girl, Buddy," she crooned. "You're safe."

Sam slung her arm over Buddy's neck, brushing her fingers over the plush red fur. The calf trembled.

As she looked up at Ross, Sam wondered if he was shaking, too. She'd never met anyone so shy. Ross's downcast eyes told Sam she might have a better chance getting an answer from Tank, Ross's flop-eared bay horse.

"What happened?" Sam asked.

"Got out," Ross mumbled.

Sam nearly laughed. It had cost the big cowboy so much to tell her what she already knew.

"It's a good thing I came along when I did," Sam said.

The cowboy nodded. "Want a rope?" He touched the lariat coiled and strapped to his saddle.

"If you go ahead of us, back to the ranch, I think

she'll follow me in," Sam said.

Without a word, Ross spun the cow pony away.

In appreciation, Buddy rubbed her muzzle against Sam's white shirt. Sam looked down at the smear of grassy slobber.

"Yeah, you're welcome," Sam said.

She finished the long walk home with the calf tagging along at her side.

At dinner, Gram and Dad asked endless questions about her first day of school.

"English, history, and journalism, I feel fine about," Sam told them. "And I had a good Spanish teacher last year in San Francisco."

"That will be a help," Gram said, passing Sam another slice of the whole wheat bread she'd baked that afternoon. "Did you see Maxine Ely?"

"She's my history teacher," Sam said. "She must have recognized me. She sort of smiled when she called my name during roll."

"She's a good woman," Dad said, but he sounded preoccupied.

"Don't you have a few other classes?" Gram insisted.

Sam knew what Gram was asking. During the last two years, when they'd communicated by letters, Sam hadn't been shy in telling Gram she was a terrible, hopeless, thick-headed math student.

"P.E. and algebra," Sam admitted.

In fact, she dreaded her gym class almost as much as math class. Darton High required students to shower after gym. Both Rachel and Daisy were in Sam's P.E. class, and she had no desire to stand in the same locker room with those beauty queens.

"You be sure to ask for extra help in algebra," Gram said, "if you need it."

Sam knew she'd need it. Still, she couldn't help being irritated that Gram was waiting for her to fail.

A wave of weariness washed over Sam. She stifled a yawn. She had finished the first two chapters in her journalism book during study hall, so her only other homework was to cover her textbooks. After that, she wanted to climb into bed.

"Buddy got out again," Dad said.

Sam's weariness vanished as if Dad had tossed a bucket of water her way. "I know. I caught her."

"Next time, you might not," Dad said.

"I don't think—" Sam began.

"Now, hush," Gram said. "It wasn't your fault. That calf's just trying to do what's natural. She wants to be with the other cattle."

Most of the other cattle will die soon, Sam thought.

"But Buddy's different," Sam said. "Dad told me so, just this morning." Sam stared at her father for confirmation.

"I did," Dad said. "But that doesn't mean I'm softheaded."

"Just softhearted," Gram said, looking amused.

Dad ignored her. "Buddy needs branding."

Sam shivered, remembering the smell of the small fire of dried sagebrush and the sound of white-hot branding irons clinking against each other. As a child, the stink of burning hair hadn't bothered her as much as the bleating of the calves. She'd imagined they were crying to their mothers.

Now, she was Buddy's mother.

"It's going to hurt," Sam said, wincing.

"It always does," Dad said, "but just for a minute and not nearly as much as getting caught up with someone else's herd and butchered."

That was the point of a brand. Thousands of red, white-faced cattle wandered the range. Even when they were gathered together, they were impossible to tell apart. Cowboys might remember a steer with a crumpled horn or a cow freckled with white, but such differences were rare.

A brand guaranteed each rancher moved his own cattle to summer pasture.

"If you're serious about keeping her," Dad added, "we should do an ear mark, too. That way riders can see who she belongs to from horseback, when the herd's packed together tight."

"I'm serious about keeping her," Sam said.

"We'll do it this weekend." Dad pushed his chair back from the table. Sam heard him plop into his recliner in the living room.

Sam felt the prickle of tears. Sure, Dad could just

go off and forget. Branding Buddy meant nothing to him.

She knew it had to be done to protect Buddy, but when they seared the calf's skin with a branding iron, they were burning her and creating a scar.

"You know," Gram said, as the television clicked on in the other room, "it would only take him a few minutes to brand Buddy while you were at school. He's waiting for the weekend so you can comfort her when it's over."

"I know," Sam said. "And I know it has to be done, but I don't have to like it."

By the time she finished washing dishes, dusk had fallen, but Sam still went out to visit Buddy.

Buddy didn't want to visit. In the middle of the pasture, she stopped grazing, looked at Sam, and flicked her tail as if shooing a pesky fly. She turned her attention back to the grass.

"Okay for you," Sam muttered, then walked toward the small corral beside the barn.

Ace nickered when he saw her coming.

"No carrots," Sam confessed, holding her palms open as she approached.

Sweetheart blew through her lips and shuffled away from the fence rails, but Ace remained.

He looked a little scruffy. Since she hadn't ridden him today, she hadn't brushed him, and the little mustang loved the massage of the rubber brush.

"You are spoiled, you know." Sam led him into the barn, turned on the light, and began grooming.

As she brushed, Sam turned from telling the bay gelding how pretty he was, to confiding her worries. She could tell Ace her troubles and not worry that he'd tell anyone else.

"I suppose I should ask Jake about the blue roan," she murmured to Ace. "I want to, but he'll think of some reason to worry. He's so protective, you'd think he was my brother."

Sam smoothed the brush along Ace's back, thinking. The hammer-head stallion was young, but he had a broad chest and the muscled haunches of a mature horse.

Sam had seen small bands of bachelor stallions cast out of their herds as potential challengers to the ruling stallion. But they tended to be gangly youngsters.

Sam would bet the hammer head was at least three years old. He might have lost his harem of mares to another stallion, or maybe they'd been captured in one of the BLM's wild horse gathers.

When Ace stamped, Sam realized she'd been so deep in thought, she'd stopped brushing.

"Sorry," she told the gelding. "But the more I think about him, the more I believe Hammer is trouble."

Ace swung his head around and his eyes met hers.

"That's what I've been calling him in my head," Sam explained. "Hammer, because of his big head and the way he kicked that fence."

Ace's brown eyes stayed fixed on her, as if he expected more. "That's not silly, is it?"

Ace bobbed his head, and his forelock fell away from the white star on his forehead.

"Too bad," Sam said, laughing, but she didn't give Hammer another thought until morning.

Sam and Jen were waiting for the bus when a baby blue Mercedes-Benz swished past, carrying Rachel Slocum to school.

"Wave to the princess," Jen said, lifting her arm so high, her raspberry tee shirt cleared the top of her jeans.

Sam loved Jen Kenworthy's sarcasm, but as she stared after the car, she pictured the mansion at Gold Dust Ranch. The Mercedes must have passed within yards of the foreman's house.

"I can't believe they'd drive right past your house and not give you a ride to school." Sam took the snub personally. "What do they think," she sputtered, "you—you've got cooties?"

"Don't bring out the elementary school insults on my account," Jen said, but her eyes sparkled behind her glasses. "I mean, I *am* just the foreman's daughter. The housekeeper wouldn't expect to drive me to school. Besides, Rachel and I don't exactly belong to the same clique."

"I don't care," Sam said.

"Linc told my mom that Rachel rides alone, because she can't be distracted. She uses the drive into Darton to do her homework."

Jen twirled the end of one blond braid. Though she smiled, Sam could tell Jen didn't like being shunned.

"Home. Work." Sam pronounced the words slowly. "Do you think Rachel hasn't quite figured out the concept?"

Jen gave her a grateful grin. "I don't want to be her friend, anyway. In fact, if Dad didn't love the ranch so much, and it weren't for the horses, I'd like to move."

"I believe you."

"You know, when Linc Slocum had his well drilled, it ended up draining too much water from ours. My mom can't do laundry some days and we have to be careful when we take showers."

"Did you tell him?"

"My dad did, but that was over a year ago. Nothing's changed and I don't expect it will." Jen shrugged. "He had a bulldozer scrape dirt into a pile, so he could be king of the mountain, where there wasn't even a molehill before!

"Every night before sunset, that huge house casts a shadow over ours." Jen's voice faded to a whisper. "I don't like living in Slocum's shadow."

A crow glided overhead, cawing. Jen looked up and pulled the neck of her tee shirt to cover her lips.

"You're right," she called after the bird. "Blah, blah, blah."

Sam bit her lip. Everything Jen said made Sam like her more. They valued the same things. Since she'd come home from San Francisco, she'd learned that sunsets were more important than fancy houses.

She needed to cheer Jen up.

"Speaking of homework, do you know how to work that fancy calculator of yours?" Sam pointed to the complex grid of buttons and arrows showing through the mesh pocket on Jen's backpack.

Sam could tell by the sudden glow on Jen's face that she'd hit the right topic.

"How to work it? To put it humbly, my dear Samantha"—Jen made a mock bow—"I am a math goddess. My mom quit home schooling me because I passed her in geometry when I was in fifth grade. This year I'm taking calculus."

"I'm taking algebra for dummies," Sam told her.

Jen tilted her head to one side, and sunlight glazed the lenses of her glasses.

"You can't be taking honors English and remedial math."

"Yes, I can," Sam said, surprised she didn't mind exposing her shortcomings to her new friend. "I am truly *un*gifted with numbers."

"Well, girl," Jen said, giving her a playful punch in the arm, "today's your lucky day."

Chapter Nine ⁊

Sam's first week of school almost ended well.

She'd been on time for each class. She'd turned in every bit of homework. She liked her teachers, especially Mrs. Ely and Mr. Blair. She'd interviewed the principal, Ms. Santos, and discovered she had humor and a flair for lively language that made writing the interview easy. RJay, *Dialogue*'s editor in chief, read the story and flashed Sam a thumbs-up.

And Sam's locker only jammed once.

The week had grown hotter each day, and no rain was predicted. Dad went about his work with a smile, getting ready to pounce on the one-hundred-degree day when it dawned.

As Jake had said weeks ago, the fall roundup paled in comparison to the cattle drive to summer pasture or the spring roundup. In a single day, the steers vanished off the home range, and Dad shipped them off to market with Dallas, the gray-haired foreman, as escort. Now, Dad waited for the final tally saying how much they'd earned from the range-fed Herefords.

Best of all, Dad said Sam could ride, come Sunday. The announcement launched her into a dozen daydreams of taking Ace out over the foothills with Jen and her palomino.

In all, the week had been great, except Sam *did* wish Jake hadn't been so busy. With the beginning of school, things had been bound to change, but she was surprised by how much she missed him.

Her spirits lightened, though, when she remembered Jake's birthday. It was still six weeks away but Sam knew she could count on Gram to do something special, even if they couldn't afford an expensive gift.

Standing at the bus stop on Friday morning, Sam wore a sleeveless blue blouse, but she was already flushed and warm. Dozens of mouse-colored clouds hovered overhead, but they didn't offer the coolness of shade. They just made the morning dark.

Sam pulled the collar away from her neck as she and Jen planned a ride to War Drum Flats.

The bus was coming. The girls settled their backpacks in place as the diesel huff of the bus drew near. The familiar sound was interrupted by a sudden squeal of tires and screeching of brakes.

The murky sky made the car's headlights glare red-gold. The lights veered from side to side, as if pushed by a demonic wind. Sam recognized the car.

Linc Slocum gunned his Cadillac until it lurched within feet of the bus's back bumper. He swerved into the lane for oncoming traffic, then angled across the bus's path and sped forward, toward Jen and Sam.

Sam's hand flew up to cover her lips. Her pulse beat in her wrists and ankles, even behind her knees, as her heart pounded out a warning. Jen looked suddenly pale, but joked through her fear.

She shaded her eyes and squinted at Slocum's car. "As my daddy would say, 'There's a man mad enough to kick a hog.'"

Sam tried to answer in kind. "I can't repeat what my dad would say if he saw Slocum cutting off a school bus."

If only Dad were here.

The bus pulled up beside the Cadillac as Slocum climbed out and rounded the front of his car. The bus driver opened the bus door and shouted, but Slocum paid no attention. He stormed toward the girls, shaking his fist.

In the instant before she understood Slocum's words, Sam saw faces press against the bus window, watching.

"That renegade, that mongrel, that *mutt* of a horse has trespassed—" Slocum took a loud breath, as if the morning air held too little oxygen for his ranting "—on my property. That menace has ruined my investment—"

He must be talking about the Phantom. Had the

mustang destroyed a fence or some rosebushes? What was Slocum yelling about? And why was his shirt buttoned crooked and his jeans hanging over bare ankles and bedroom slippers?

"Mr. Slocum," Jen said quietly. "We don't know what you're talking about."

Slocum kept his back to Jen. He loomed over Sam. She saw sweat beaded on his upper lip, and she heard bus windows slamming open so everyone could listen. Oh, great.

With his fingers formed like a child pretending he held a gun, Slocum yelled, "*You* know what I'm talking about. This time it's not some cow pony your silver menace stole. Apache Hotspot is the cornerstone of *my* new breeding program." Slocum's fist struck his chest when he said *my*. "That mare's the investment of a lifetime!"

Finally, Sam understood. Slocum hadn't just purchased the sweet chocolate-and-white Appaloosa as a gift for Rachel. The mare was an investment. And she was gone.

"I want you to call that stud! Call the Phantom!"

Past Slocum, Sam saw Jen's jaw drop in amazement.

Good. Let everyone on the bus see how insane Slocum was. She couldn't call the Phantom. Not really.

"Mr. Slocum, I'm really sorry your horse is —"

"Don't give me that," he snarled. "I want that

mustang down here, now!" Slocum's face was twisted with rage. Any second now, he was going to burst a blood vessel.

Sam shrugged out of her backpack and let it drop. There was no place to hide, but she was darn sure she could outrun Slocum. She'd done it before.

From inside the bus, there came a sound like a telephone receiver slamming down. The bus driver tramped down the stairs, and the sound of his approach made Slocum glance back.

"Thank goodness," Jen whispered.

"Sir? I've radioed the sheriff," said the driver. "I think you'd better get back in your car and wait for him."

"The sheriff? Of all the idiotic—" Slocum stopped blustering and took a breath. "Guess I did get a little loco, didn't I? Shucks, when a man works hard and sinks his money into a fine piece of horseflesh, it's just downright disappointing to lose it."

Sam shivered. Slocum was talking like a Hollywood cowpoke. The sudden change was spookier than his clenched fist.

The bus driver looked confused, but he motioned the girls toward the safety of the bus and held his other arm out, barring Slocum from following.

The bus swayed as students returned to seats on the opposite side of the bus. Both Sam and Jen noticed and met each other's eyes. Sam hesitated before stepping up.

"There are at least twenty kids on that bus," Sam whispered wildly to Jen. "If each of them gets off at school and tells one person what they saw, that's forty people who know, and if each of them goes to class and tells—"

"I can do the math, Sam. You're right, they'll gossip. But we didn't do anything wrong. We're the victims—or, nearly were—of Rachel's nutty father." Jen flinched as Slocum's car door slammed. "The man doesn't do well when he doesn't get his way."

Sam remembered Slocum's rage when Brynna wouldn't allow him to adopt the Phantom. Jen was right.

They spotted an empty seat about eight rows back from the front of the bus. Jen and Sam took it. For a minute, all was quiet. The bus doors closed. The driver put the vehicle into gear and pulled back onto the road.

Sam kept her eyes focused on the seat back in front of her, until a boy across the aisle poked her arm.

"Hey, what was wrong with him?"

Sam shrugged. "I guess he lost his horse."

From the corner of her eye, Sam saw Jen smile, but then an avalanche of questions began.

"Was he crazy?"

"Was he talking about the Phantom?"

"Did he think the Phantom stole something?"

"Yeah, like a ghost cares about mortal mares."

That speaker wore glasses and pushed them back up his nose in a superior fashion.

Sam's relief froze. Did everyone know the legend? She racked her brain for a clever answer.

"I don't know," she said.

A girl with a pierced nostril turned in the seat just ahead. Sam searched her mind for the girl's name. Callie, that was it. The girl was in her Spanish class.

"It sounded like he thought you were a witch," Callie said. "Like you could conjure the stallion to come to you."

"Now *that's* crazy talk," Jen said.

"But she is from San Francisco," Callie pointed out.

Jen laughed. "They carry briefcases there, Callie, not magic wands."

The remark got a laugh. As the tension around her evaporated, Sam looked at her watch. She shook her wrist. Sam couldn't believe it was only eight o'clock.

Sam took the glass of lemonade Gram handed her as she walked into the kitchen after school. She felt light-headed and weird after the long hot walk home but not so weird she didn't notice four unbaked pies and six pans of lasagna crowded side by side on the kitchen counter. Oddest of all was Gram's expression.

"What's wrong?" Sam asked. She held the glass against her cheek instead of drinking.

"The check Dallas brought home for the cattle wasn't much," Gram said. "We barely broke even."

Sam sipped the lemonade.

"What does that mean?" she asked. "That we can't pay back the loans from last year?"

Gram nodded. "We'll talk tonight. Your dad's doing that last cutting of alfalfa with the hands. He left a message on the Elys' phone, too, hoping Jake and his brothers can help. Wyatt's worried it will start pouring and hurt the hay."

"*Pouring?* It's like an oven out there," Sam said. "Dad wanted a one-hundred-degree day and this is it."

"Look at that sky, young lady." Gram pointed toward the window. "It's tight as the head of a drum. The weather stations say this is a window between two storms."

"If it starts to rain now, is the hay ruined?"

"Not necessarily. Once the hay is cut and baled, a single hot day can dry it," Gram said. "Your dad's got it cut. If they can get it baled today, we might be all right."

Gram sipped her own lemonade before adding, "I just hope my old granny wasn't right. She said when hens left off laying for no good reason, they were predicting hailstorms."

Sam rubbed her hand across her eyes. She'd really wanted to tell Gram what had happened this morning.

The halls had been abuzz before Sam even

reached her first period class. By second period, people were outright staring at her and Jen. When Rachel Slocum had left school "sick," everyone pitied poor Rachel, whose father was a lunatic. By the time her last class began, Sam had heard gossip saying he'd run the school bus off the road into a ditch.

With rumors flying, Sam longed to tell Gram the truth before she heard something worse. But Gram and Dad were fretting over money and weather and saving the hay crop. This might not be the best time to mention she hadn't had such a great day either.

"If I don't put on shorts, I'll pass out." Sam stood up and headed toward her bedroom, but stopped before she reached the stairs. "I bet there's something I should be doing to help."

"See to the animals, then come help me cook." Gram gestured toward the pans of lasagna. "The cowboys will eat here tonight, and if the Elys come, that makes seven extra men for dinner. Even with a small cutting, they'll work up an appetite." Gram fanned herself with a dish towel.

Sam had jogged halfway up the stairs when she heard Gram mutter, "And I don't know where I'll find the strength to turn on that oven."

Buddy didn't seem to think the storm would hold off another day. Or maybe she'd picked up on Sam's worry over the branding.

The calf mooed and pressed against the fence

rails, trying to follow Sam as she did chores. When the skies darkened and a tumbleweed skittered across the yard, Buddy bucked and bawled, certain the weed had blown in off the range to devour her.

Finally, Sam put Buddy inside the barn. Sam was scattering extra straw in the box stall when she heard a truck.

Sam sprinted outside. Jake was alone in the truck. Maybe he'd already dropped his brothers at the hay field. It didn't matter. All week she'd wanted to ask Jake if he'd rope Buddy tomorrow for the branding. Not only was he skillful with the lariat, Jake would be gentle.

If she said that, he'd be embarassed.

Jake reached inside the truck for his Stetson. Ready for hot-weather work, he wore a sleeveless white undershirt and jeans. As he pulled his Stetson down low, Sam saw the wind catch the long hair he'd tamed with a leather thong. He slammed the door of the pickup and glanced toward the house but kept walking her way.

Sam swallowed hard. This was really stupid. She shouldn't be so glad to see Jake. Or so uneasy. When he got close enough to take her in a one-armed bear hug and walk her back inside the barn, she was happier than she'd been all week.

Jake bumped up the brim of his hat to get a better look at her. "So, how was your mornin', Brat?"

"You heard?" she asked, though she doubted

anyone at Darton High hadn't.

"Do I have ears?" Jake waited, thumbs hooked in his belt loops.

"Linc Slocum is not a healthy man," she said.

"He's a real self-centered son of a gun." Jake stared at the barn floor as he spoke. "I know that for a fact, but don't tell me he laid a hand on you or Jen."

When Jake looked up, his eyes were hard.

"He didn't," Sam said quickly.

"Good thing."

Sam didn't ask why. She could figure it out for herself. Though their parents didn't approve, the Ely boys had reputations for settling disputes with their fists.

With a yap of greeting, Blaze bounded into the barn. He stood next to Jake, bumping against his leg, inviting a pat. Jake slid his hand down the dog's back, then straightened.

"My brothers are helping your dad. My dad will be along soon. I better hightail it down there." Jake didn't move, though his boot heels creaked as his weight shifted.

"I've got to help Gram make garlic biscuits to go with the lasagna." Sam didn't know what she was waiting for. Then, she blurted, "We're supposed to brand Buddy tomorrow."

"There's no cause to be sentimental over that." Jake squared his shoulders and looked down on her like he had since she was five years old.

"It's not that I'm sentimental over Buddy," she tried to explain. "It's all this other stuff."

Jake brushed her off with a single word, "Yeah," he said. "Gotta go."

He did.

Sam held Blaze's collar to keep him from following. As he started the truck and drove off, Sam sent a frown after Jake.

"Thanks for nothing, you turkey." Sam released the dog's collar, made sure Buddy's stall was latched, and headed for the house.

Hot wind spun the dust from Jake's tires in a whirlwind. It danced across the ranch yard, causing horses to pin back their ears in warning.

Chapter Ten ல

𝒯HE HAILSTORM STARTED and ended before dark.

While Gram showered, Sam put two pans of biscuits in to bake. First, she heard a pinging sound, then a tapping, next a rattling like machine-gun fire in a movie.

Sam hurried to the window. In the ten-acre pasture, the horses galloped like a wild herd. Heads and tails flung high, they raced around the pasture as if trying to outrun the hail. For five minutes, ice pellets showered from the sky, bouncing like Ping-Pong balls as they hit the ground. Minutes later, the storm stopped, leaving the evening sky blue-gold and scoured clean.

"Is something burning?" Gram called from upstairs.

Sam jerked the biscuits from the oven, then waited for Gram to tell her what the hailstorm would mean for the hay.

"Not good." Gram rushed into the kitchen in a pink gingham blouse and fresh jeans. She tugged one end of the kitchen table and added another leaf to make it longer. "Not good at all, but Wyatt should have it baled by now, and he's got tarps to cover the hay. It won't dry out there now. He'll just have to bring it in and feed it. Or sell it right away."

With company coming for dinner, Sam wanted to change out of the red tank top and white shorts she'd put on after school. But there was no time.

All of a sudden, trucks came roaring in, and men in cowboy hats were everywhere.

Sam lifted the kitchen curtain just enough to watch them wash up outside and use a big purple first aid kit from the Elys' truck to bandage one of Jake's brother's hand. Their voices drifted through the open window.

"Whoee, that thing's so purple, it could blind a man," Dallas joked.

"Yeah," said Luke, Jake's father. "But if a man needs a first aid kit, he doesn't want to spend all day looking for it."

When the men began stomping mud off their boots on the front porch, Sam moved away from the window just in time. All at once a cluster of men followed Dad inside. Each hung his hat on the hat rack, until it was full. Then they used the coat rack.

Sam hustled between the stove and the table,

carrying the full platters Gram handed her. She slipped into her chair just before Dad said grace, but her eyes were only half closed. Dad's forehead furrowed as he thanked God for the food and the safety of the men who'd helped with haying. While Dad prayed, Dallas rubbed his temples and sighed.

Then, like a scene from a movie, the subdued meal was devoured to the clatter of knives and forks. In those movies, the farm wife didn't sit down and eat, but Gram pulled up a chair long before the meal ended.

Sam wanted to catch Jake's eye and get a feel for just how serious things were, but each time she tried, Jake's brothers noticed. So did his father.

Luke was a handsome but harsh-looking man. He didn't say a word during dinner, but Sam couldn't help studying him. The smooth sheen of his skin made Sam aware of the clean shelf of his cheekbones and smooth length of his jaw. He had more sharp edges than Jake, but when Sam brought him pie and coffee, Luke's smile made her grin right back.

As if the smile loosened his long-boned jaw, Luke said, "I could use some of that hay if you come up with extra."

Dad's mouth lifted at one corner, but the expression wasn't a smile. Why not? Sam wondered. Dad needed to use or sell the hay before it spoiled.

"Thanks, Luke." Dad sounded as if Luke had offered a favor.

"I haven't shipped my herd yet. You raise high-protein feed. I could use some," Luke repeated.

One of Jake's brothers, the one with the bandaged hand, spoke next. "I have a friend who trains jumpers up at Lake Tahoe. She's always looking for high-quality hay. I could drive some up to her, if you can spare it."

"Go ahead and call her," Dad said. He held a fork, but he hadn't yet cracked the crust of his pie. "If the flatbed can make it up there, that'd be fine."

Dad flushed. While the other men talked, he stayed quiet. Sam didn't understand, until the Elys rose to leave.

Sam blinked at all the tall browned men. It was as if a redwood forest had sprouted in the kitchen.

The boys walked ahead, but Dad paused in the doorway and shook Luke Ely's hand.

"It's not so humiliatin' when you're bailed out by good friends," Dad said.

Luke shrugged. "Don't know what you're talking about, Wyatt. You're the one doin' me a favor."

It was easy to see Luke's generosity and know that when the time came, Dad would help the Elys, too.

The brothers clambered into the truck bed, haggling for the best seats, and Sam hoped only Jake would hear her.

"Jake?" She tried to call quietly, but all the Elys looked.

Even though there were no lights in the ranch

yard, Sam's white shorts made her all too visible. Jake's brothers elbowed him, joshed him, and one mimicked Sam, calling his name in a high voice. All the same, Jake walked with solid steps back to meet her.

"Yeah?" he said, holding his hat and looking at her sideways, as if she'd scold him.

"Could I ask you a favor, please?"

He nodded with long-suffering patience.

"I've been thinking about this all evening, kind of rehearsing, so I don't do anything dumb like cry," Sam said. "Tomorrow, when we brand Buddy, could you—do you mind—?" Sam stopped, made a smoothing motion with her hands as if steadying her mind was that easy. "Would you please be the one to rope Buddy?"

Sam remembered the way a rider roped the calf's two hind legs, then dragged her the short distance to the branding fire. Done correctly, it was quick. But Sam had seen ropers catch only one hoof or lasso the calf's tail along with a leg. Often, horses took a while to get into position, and cowboys ended up chasing the calf until it was terrified.

But not Witch and Jake. Together, they were a synchronized roping team. She trusted them.

"Why me?" Jake asked.

"Because you'll get it right the first time," Sam said. Jake looked bashful, and she was afraid he'd refuse out of modesty.

"Because if you do it," Sam added, "Buddy won't be scared any longer than she has to be."

Jake groaned.

"Samantha, you drive me crazy." Jake shook his head and glared at the night sky as if the stars ought to help him out. "What if I miss?"

"You won't!" Sam took two light steps away. His disgusted expression said she'd better escape before he changed his mind.

From the front porch steps, Dad called, "Fire ought to be ready by seven-thirty, Jake."

Dad had been listening all along. Drenched with embarrassment, Sam looked at Jake, spreading her hands in a gesture of helplessness.

"Yes, sir," Jake called, and he seemed just fine as he strode back to his father's truck.

Sam didn't feel fine.

"There's no privacy around this place," she said, letting the door slam behind her as she entered the kitchen. "Not a bit!"

Dad didn't look properly ashamed.

"Sure there is, honey." Gram sounded sympathetic, but her smile held some sort of trick. "Your dad and I are going into the living room to watch a little television."

Gram untied her apron, handed it to Sam, and nodded at a sink stacked high with dirty dishes. "You can have the kitchen all to yourself."

❧ ❧

Sage-spiced smoke made its way into Sam's bedroom, waking her with thoughts of branding. It was Saturday. She *could* sleep in, but then she thought of Buddy. The calf had no idea what the day held for her. Suddenly, Sam was wide awake.

She swung her feet out of bed and stood. Through her nightgown, Sam touched her hip. She'd hate to have a scar burned on her skin.

Dad expected her help. She, Dad, and Jake would do the branding. Once the iron was heated, Jake would ride into the ten-acre pasture and rope Buddy. Sam would swing open the gate, let Jake ride through with the calf, slam the gate, then run to where Dad waited with the branding iron.

Sam didn't feel like eating. She skipped breakfast and went outside. The hens fluttered at the sight of her and scurried away. Dad squatted beside a little campfire.

He didn't give orders, but Sam knew what to do. She gathered an armload of sagebrush and stacked it near the fire. After a few minutes, Sam realized she and Dad both stood with arms crossed, staring down into the flames. Dad seemed even quieter than usual, probably because of the hailstorm and lost winter fodder.

Dad scooted the business end of the branding iron into the fire. After a while, he rotated it a turn. He did that every so often, sometimes pulling it from the fire and blowing on the iron to scatter the ash. He checked the iron's progress as it turned from black to gray to red.

Sam snapped a piece of twisted gray sagebrush into small lengths and dropped them into the fire.

"That's enough," Dad said.

Sam realized she was feeding the fire to keep from imagining the searing pain from that hot iron.

From the instant Jake loped over the wooden bridge and into the ranch yard, he and Dad communicated in silence. Though they didn't wiggle their ears at each other like horses, Dad used only a few gestures to outline the plan he'd explained to Sam last night. And Jake nodded.

It was clear to Sam that both men wanted this operation over with quickly. So did Sam, but she had the feeling Dad and Jake felt embarrassed about making such a fuss over a solitary calf.

She knew they were doing it for her.

At last, Dad drew the branding iron out, blew on it, and looked up at Sam.

"That's what we've been waiting for," he said, showing her the metal had turned gray white.

As Jake limbered up his rope and Witch danced in excitement, Sam jogged to the pasture and opened the gate. The horses stopped grazing to watch Witch lope past, and Buddy glanced up. Grass fell from her lips. She looked to the horses for advice and then, bewildered, jogged where Jake herded her.

Sam blinked back tears. She refused to cry, but

Buddy's confusion made Sam's heart ache.

Closer and closer Jake herded the calf. Was he going to ride past the open gate and rope the tiny black hooves somewhere farther out? At last, just before the gate, Jake leaned forward and gently cast the loop over Buddy's hind legs. She fell almost at Sam's feet and Jake rode through, dragging her mere yards to where Dad waited.

Sam latched the gate and sprinted after them. She knelt at Buddy's head, steadying her, looking into the calf's frightened eyes.

"It's okay, Buddy," she crooned, and then there was a sizzle, a thread of pungent smoke and the branding iron was lifted.

"Go," Dad said.

The rope that was stretched tight between Buddy and Jake now slackened as Witch stepped forward.

Quick as her shaking fingers could move, Sam slipped the loop from Buddy's legs.

She rocked the calf. "You can get up, baby."

Buddy scrambled to her feet, staggered a step, then stampeded toward the barn, her tail held straight up.

"Go on after her," Dad said. "You can sleep in the barn tonight, too, if you want."

Amazed, but afraid to stay around in case he changed his mind, Sam followed Buddy.

Last night, Dad had told her that mother cows always rushed to nurse their calves after the traumatic experience of branding.

Though Buddy ate mostly grass these days, Sam had left a bottle in the box stall, just in case. What worked for other calves might work for Buddy.

It did. As soon as Sam offered the bottle, Buddy latched her lips around the nipple. She tugged and sucked, gazing up at Sam with accusing eyes.

"It's okay, baby," Sam said. "Now you won't get lost, ever."

At last, the calf's eyes closed. She drew on the nipple more slowly and her tail stopped switching from side to side. Buddy's knees buckled wearily. With a shuddering sigh like a baby who's cried itself to sleep, Buddy collapsed into the straw. Her long white eyelashes fluttered, and then she napped.

Sam felt almost like she'd been napping when she emerged from the dim barn. When she saw Dad standing with his arm around Brynna Olson, she knew she was dreaming.

From the small corral, Ace nickered.

"Tomorrow, boy," she said.

Ace stamped his hoof impatiently. For the first time since she'd come home, Sam didn't answer the gelding's summons. She had to see what was going on with Dad and Brynna.

A quick glance showed her the white BLM truck. Another look, as she walked closer, showed Sam her imagination had run away with her.

Dad's arm lay along the top fence rail, *not* around Brynna Olson. Still, Brynna stood pretty close. She was talking to Dad and having to look up at him. Dad was looking down and listening intently.

Sam paused next to the big flatbed truck Dad had pulled out of the barn. She wasn't spying on them, exactly, or even hiding. She just happened to stop and tie her shoe where they wouldn't see her.

Sam crouched there, listening. The conversation she overheard was definitely not romantic.

"Wyatt, I do believe you're the most bullheaded man I've met," said Brynna Olson. "This is a great job, with a terrific salary, using horseman's skills you've mastered. Your contract would run from November to March—months your cattle pretty much take care of themselves—and still, you turn me down."

Brynna had gone from leaning on the fence beside Dad to standing in front of him, hands on her hips.

"Just tell me why," Brynna demanded.

"I work for myself—no one else," Dad said. "And for darn sure, not for the government."

Brynna threw her hands in the air with a strangled little scream of frustration. Sam covered her mouth, smothering a giggle. She'd never heard an adult make that particular sound, but she knew exactly how Brynna felt.

Dad's jaw was set hard, and he wore his stubborn-mule face. No one would be able to budge him.

"Part of this is selfish," Brynna admitted. "I need to go to Washington for some meetings. I'd like everything *not* to fall apart while I'm gone." She tilted her head to one side, as if she were talking to a small child or a smart dog. And she waited.

"Yeah," Dad said.

"Someone from Las Vegas will fill in for me while I'm gone." Brynna let that sink in for a minute. "I don't want my replacement to hand this wrangler's position over to some dude who doesn't know how to ride, or worse, some yahoo who treats horses like machines!"

Brynna was so wound up, she missed it, but Sam saw Dad nearly laugh out loud. That was why he was nodding, all serious, as he looked down at the boot he was scuffing in the dirt. Yep, Dad thought *yahoo* was pretty funny.

"You know, Brynna—" Dad began.

Whoa. When had Dad started calling Miss Olson, Brynna?

"—I appreciate the offer, but you're not going to change my mind."

"Because it's a government job."

"Because it's working for somebody else."

Sam couldn't figure Dad out. Had he forgotten about the hailstorm, about the drought-thin cattle that sold for next to nothing, about the school clothes and horse vaccinations and windmill parts he couldn't afford?

Out of nowhere, a hand clamped over Sam's mouth. A strong arm jerked her backward. She slammed down on the seat of her jeans in the dust. And then she was looking up into Jake's mischievous brown eyes.

She tried to shake her lips loose from his hand as he whispered, "Getting yourself quite an earful, Brat?"

Chapter Eleven ∽

"WHAT ARE YOU kids doing?" Dad's voice boomed like an explosion, when their scuffling drew his attention.

"You are so dead," Sam said. Since she barely breathed the words, Sam wasn't certain Jake heard, but she'd bet her eyes were shooting fire. Even Jake wasn't too dense to understand *that*.

Together, they stood. Sam waved, but Dad didn't look amused. By the time they walked within range, Brynna Olson saved them from making excuses. Brynna knew they'd been eavesdropping. She showed it by blushing to the roots of her red hair, but she refused to let her humiliation last.

"You two know about Slocum's Appaloosa, I suppose."

"Yeah," Jake said. "I've seen rails down on his fences. She could've been restless in her new corral and walked off."

"It's possible," Brynna said.

"I know Slocum thinks the Phantom stole her," Sam said, "but it wasn't him."

"Just how do you know what Linc Slocum's thinking?" Dad said the words slowly, warning Sam he wasn't happy.

"He, uh, talked to me at the bus stop yesterday."

"So I heard." Dad's voice dropped even lower. "I don't like being the last to know an adult threatened my daughter."

"He didn't. Not really. He never said he'd hurt me," Sam assured her father. "He just loomed over me and Jen. He had the crazy idea I could whistle and the Phantom would come running."

Although no one turned to look, Sam was pretty sure Jake, Brynna, and Dad were listening to the river rushing nearby, remembering she'd met the Phantom there, more than once.

"I wanted to tell you and Gram." Sam defended herself. "But things were complicated yesterday—with the haying and storm and ten people for dinner."

"Doesn't matter," Dad said. "If he—if *anyone*—does something like that again, I want to know about it. No matter what."

"All right," Sam said.

There was a moment's silence before Brynna spoke.

"Of course, Slocum wants the Bureau to catch the horse. He called yesterday, after his chat with Sheriff

Ballard." Brynna hid her smile. "He demanded I catch this renegade stallion. In all probability it *is* a mustang, and I'm trying to hire a wrangler to trap the stud." Brynna brushed a wisp of red hair back toward her French braid. "But I'm not having much luck."

The Phantom probably wasn't to blame, but if it did turn out to be him, Sam couldn't hope for a better captor than Dad. If Dad trapped the Phantom, he'd treat him with respect, not violence.

Sam glanced Dad's way. As if he could read her mind, he crossed his arms. Tight.

Brynna Olson probably had a better chance of changing Dad's mind than Sam did. The best thing she could do was vanish and hope they worked it out.

"Dad, is it okay if I go to Alkali with Jake to pick up some chick-scratch?" Sam noticed, from the corner of her eye, that Jake looked completely confused, so she rushed on. "Gram forgot to get it when we were in Darton buying school clothes and . . ."

"Go ahead." Dad extracted several dollar bills from his wallet. Sam had started picturing cheeseburgers at Clara's coffee shop when he said, "Gas money. That Buick drinks like a fish."

"Thanks," Sam said.

She was leading a baffled Jake away when she heard Brynna say something softly. As always, conversation that sounded like a secret caught Sam's attention.

"That's assuming it was a horse that stole his new Appaloosa."

"Wasn't it?" Dad asked.

"Slocum made a big show of buying that mare and having her delivered in a horse van that cost a thousand dollars a day. He pointed out that Sam had talked with the driver about the Appaloosa's registration and pedigree."

"Don't tell me he thinks Sam had anything to do—?"

Even though it was a bad idea to interrupt her father, Sam couldn't stop.

"*What?*" Sam whipped around and marched back toward the two adults.

"Samantha, eavesdropping is a nasty habit," Dad cautioned. "You rarely hear anything good about yourself."

"But wait—now I'm a *horse thief*?"

"Sam." Brynna used a soothing tone. "It was mentioned in anger. I don't think Mr. Slocum is going anywhere with the idea."

"He'd better not!" Sam's pulse pounded in her temples. "I'll—I'll—"

To save her from figuring out what she'd do to Linc Slocum, Jake snagged Sam's elbow and tugged her toward Gram's boat of a Buick.

"Sit in the car and polish your six-shooter, Calamity Jane. I'll go get the car keys from your grandma."

෨෬෨

It turned out Sam wasn't the only one Linc Slocum had threatened. The Phantom had a price on his head.

In Alkali, Jake and Sam split up to do errands, but they discovered Slocum's campaign against the stallion almost at the same time.

Jake saw the first wanted poster as he paid for a bag of chicken food at Phil's Fill-Up. After reading the poster, Jake hurried from the store, slung the burlap bag into the Buick's trunk, then rushed to tell Sam.

He found her right where she was supposed to be, in Clara's coffee shop buying sodas and french fries to go.

A bell jingled as he entered the diner, but Sam didn't notice. She stood reading another wanted poster taped next to the cash register.

A full-color picture of Apache Hotspot topped the poster. Sam finished staring at it to glance at Jake and then began to read the print aloud.

"'Five thousand dollar reward for information leading to safe recovery of Apache Hotspot, three-year-old running Appaloosa mare, white with liver chestnut markings.'" Sam grabbed Jake by the shoulders and tried to give him a shake.

"I know," he said, glancing at Clara, who stood at the open cash register, ready to take payment for the food. "I saw—"

Sam released her grip and tapped the bottom half of the poster, illustrated with a charcoal sketch of a rearing wild horse that looked just like the Phantom.

"But wait," she said. "He can advertise for his own horse. What he *can't* do, is this." Sam read, "'Five thousand dollar additional reward for capture of stallion implicated in theft of aforementioned mare.'"

"Honey, you gonna give me that money or stand there clutchin' it all day?" Clara tugged the dollar bills peeking from the fist Sam had crumpled them in as she read the poster.

"Oh, yeah." Sam surrendered the money. "Sorry."

Jake carried the fries and sodas toward the door.

Sam followed, her mind spinning with questions.

Wasn't it illegal for Slocum to distribute or put up that poster? What would Slocum do with the Phantom once he had him? Turn him over to BLM for relocation?

Sam stopped in the middle of the sidewalk, remembering what Slocum had said. BLM wouldn't relocate a known troublemaker. BLM would shoot him.

"Sit." Jake nodded at a wooden bench in the sunshine.

"I'm not your dog," Sam reminded him.

"True, but you're walking like a zombie. Dr. Jake's fat, salt, and sugar diet ought to fix you up."

Sam ate.

She worried about Buddy.

She drained her soda.

She watched three cars cruise down Alkali's main street.

She saw a cat on a fence post clean her paws and whiskers.

After all that, she knew what they were going to do.

"I've got a plan," Sam said, using a fry to pick up a few stray crystals of salt.

"I was afraid of that."

Sam turned to see why Jake's voice sounded muffled. He leaned back on the bench, Stetson pulled down to cover his eyes.

She couldn't believe it. Nearly every rancher around here was broke. They'd all try to win that money from Slocum before BLM stopped him from handing it out. The cruel, old-fashioned mustanging tricks would be used in secret, if the price was right. How could Jake take a nap when the Phantom's life was at stake?

Sam snatched his Stetson.

"I'm awake." Jake sat up, blinking. "I could hear you getting yourself all worked up, Samantha. So, what's your plan?"

"First, we'll call Brynna and tell her what Slocum's doing. This encourages people to do the same kind of harassment of wild horses that kept Slocum from being able to adopt a mustang, right?"

"You know she's left River Bend by now, and it's Saturday. The Willow Springs office won't be open.

Do you have her home phone number?"

Sam glared at Jake. "No, but I'll call her Monday. Anyway, here's part two. You and I will find that stallion."

"Super." Jake grabbed his hat off her lap. "I'm sure the idea hasn't crossed anybody else's mind."

"Jake, why are you giving me a hard time?"

"I'm not, Sam. Just trying to offer a little common sense. Besides, I'm surprised you want him caught. You're the one who convinced Brynna to let him go." Jake gave a disappointed shrug. "Guess it is a lot of money."

"Do you think I'd sell him out for money?" Sam crumpled the cardboard french fry container.

Insulted and angry, she stormed down the sidewalk to a trash barrel. When Jake didn't come after her, she walked back.

"I wouldn't sell *you* out for money," she told him. "And you deserve it."

Jake considered her words as if she'd spoken in another language. "I don't know what that means," Jake said.

"Never mind." Sam sighed. "The point is, the stallion Slocum wants isn't the Phantom. It's Hammer."

Once Jake pledged silence, Sam told him about the blue roan she'd seen running along the pasture fence at River Bend. She described Hammer's attempt to take the Phantom's mares, too.

"He's the one," she said.

"You're probably right, but Slocum won't go for it. He's wanted the Phantom ever since he heard about him. This is just another way to get him."

Sam placed her hands on her knees and frowned down at the sidewalk between her shoes. Slocum had convinced himself the Phantom had Hotspot, but she had to prove him wrong. Just next to her shoe, a red ant scuttled along the hot concrete, carrying a piece of straw ten times longer than his body. If he could do that, she could do this.

"Got it," she said, smiling at Jake. "We catch them both. We track, then camp out as long as we have to, or use relays of horses to chase them. If Hotspot and Hammer are together, he's the thief, right? Slocum would have no choice but to believe us." Sam rubbed her hands together. "Then, I'll give Dad the ten thousand dollars and he won't have to worry about money for a while, and he'll be so grateful, he won't even consider grounding me again."

Sam sighed with pleasure. She held her face up to the sunlight and basked. She imagined plunking down the money for the beautiful bridle and helping Jake buckle it onto Witch's shining black head. Then she realized that even for Jake, he'd been quiet too long.

Sure enough, when she looked over, Jake was smirking.

"What?" Sam demanded.

"I just noticed this little problem you have," he said.

"Oh, really?"

"Yep. For a girl in honors English, you have this weird little sentence structure defect."

"Defect?"

"Sam"—Jake sounded sympathetic—"I'm not sure what else to call it. All along, while you're talking about stalking the stallion and catching the stallion and dragging the stallion and Hotspot back to Slocum, you're saying *we*. Then, when you reach the part about spending the reward money, all of a sudden, it's *you*."

Jake planted his hat on his head before striding to Gram's Buick.

Sam sighed. Had she really hurt Jake's feelings, or was he teasing? Sometimes she just couldn't tell.

This time, it might be better to give in, because Jake was right. She had forgotten about splitting the reward money.

Sam jogged to catch up with him. "Jake, of course we'll share. I'm sorry I forgot."

"Just thought I'd mention it," he said. "'Cause I've got my eye on something a mite more stylish than this"—he patted the top of Gram's Buick— "and five thousand dollars would make a mighty nice down payment."

She had Jake on her side, Sam thought as they drove toward home. Now, only two barriers stood between her and that $10,000: Dad and Gram.

Sam thought of the ant. Of course, she could

convince Gram and Dad that the money was worth the puny risk, but just in case she was wrong, she'd wait until tomorrow to ask.

It was a good thing she was sleeping in the barn, so she wouldn't be tempted to ask too soon.

Chapter Twelve ❧

ℐN SAM'S DREAM, the barn collapsed. Boards groaned, broke, and rained down in dagger-sharp splinters, making the horses scream.

Her eyes opened to the interior of the dark barn. Sam yelped as Buddy, struggling to her feet, stepped on her arm. By the glow of the barn's night-light, the calf stumbled away from Sam's sleeping bag and stared, trembling, at the barn door.

Horses *were* screaming. It wasn't just a nightmare. Sam huddled in her sleeping bag, afraid of any clawing thing that could so terrify the horses.

A low, guttural neigh vibrated through the night as hooves struck the small corral. A familiar whinny made Sam climb out of her sleeping bag and run toward the danger.

"Ace!" Sam struggled through the deep straw, past Buddy, and through the barn door.

Huge and light as a polar bear, a shape

sideswiped Sam. She grabbed at air, then fell as the thing crashed into the fence.

Rocks stabbed Sam's knees and she crossed her arms over her head, protecting herself, even as she begged her eyes to pierce the darkness and see what monster was scaring the horses.

Slats of woods crashed inward.

Sweetheart squealed. Heavy bodies rubbed against the fence. The low, guttural neigh mixed with Ace's clear mustang call, and Sam knew.

Hammer! The blue roan had come for Sweetheart, but Ace wouldn't let her go without a fight. Sam heard teeth clack. Ace's slim shadow rose, and by the arch of his neck she guessed the gelding's jaws closed in a savage bite on the stallion's withers. Hammer wrenched loose and wheeled away. Hooves thudded on hide. A confusion of sounds came all at once, and then there was the sound of galloping.

They swept by, two horses running. A third fought free of cracking wood and launched an awkward jump over the downed fence rails.

"Ace, no! No!"

A starred forehead swung toward her. Ace slowed, hooves stuttering on the hard-packed ranch yard. The porch light flashed on, etching him in dark silhouette.

For an instant, hesitation made Ace beautiful. His body aimed for the mountains, but his head, with delicate, inquiring ears, turned toward her.

"Get inside!" Dad yelled from the porch.

His voice held a kind of command she'd never heard before. And his hands carried a rifle.

Sam ducked inside the barn. Heartbeat battering her ribs, she flattened herself beside the doorway. Dad rarely took the rifle from the locked gun case. All the commotion must have convinced him she was in danger.

But she wasn't. And she must keep Ace safe.

"They're gone!" she yelled, so Dad had to hear her. "It's just Ace—and me!"

Outside the barn door, hooves tapped and circled. Then, just higher than Sam's head, a black shadow swung in and snorted.

"Ace, here boy," Sam reached up. Her hand grazed the flat fur of his cheek, and Ace lowered his head to nuzzle her.

Breath sweet with alfalfa, Ace's lips moved over Sam's face, then her neck. Then he nosed her hard, maybe irritated that she'd halted his headlong run into the mountains.

"You wouldn't have liked it," Sam told him. "Hammer would have hurt you if you'd tried to go with him and Sweetheart. You know that, don't you, boy?"

Nearby, Sam heard the crunch of Dad's boots. "Who're you talking to, Samantha?"

"Ace." Sam braced for the remark that she babied her horse, but the comment didn't come. "The stallion—it wasn't the Phantom. You could see that, couldn't you?"

Dad shook his head. What did that mean?

"Is he all right?" Dad extended a hand toward Ace, but the gelding shied. "Let's get some light on."

"Hush, Buddy," Sam told the bawling calf. Buddy stumbled along behind her.

"Dad, couldn't you tell it wasn't the Phantom?"

Dad crossed to a light switch and the barn brightened, but he didn't answer.

"Dad, did you see—?"

"Let's help the horse who depends on you."

Sam winced at Dad's words.

Mustangs usually took care of themselves. But when Hammer attacked, Ace had been penned, unable to use speed to escape.

She haltered Ace and stood beside him, stroking his cheek while Dad examined him. Hammer's teeth had slashed five rips on the gelding's rump.

"Just when you were all healed up," Sam said. She let Ace nibble her fingers, glad he couldn't see the new injuries over the old scars.

"They don't look bad," Dad said. "We'll clean them up and cover them with some antiseptic salve, and he'll be fine. I'm more worried about this tenderness."

Ace pulled away as Dad touched his chest.

"He was fighting to keep Sweetheart."

"I heard him." Dad straightened and kneaded the skin at the base of Ace's ears. The gelding blew breath through his lips, relaxing. "He's a good pony, this one."

Out in the yard, the Buick's engine roared to life and sped away. Sam looked at her watch. It was three o'clock in the morning and even Buddy had decided to go back to sleep.

"Where's Gram going?"

"She's going after Sweetheart." Dad sighed. "But I think that stud will herd Sweetheart clear out of here." Dad glanced after the Buick's red taillights. "I told your Gram so, but she has other ideas."

With two corral rails broken, it was safer to leave Ace inside. Dad whipped up a warm bran mash for the gelding and they left him in a box stall next to Buddy's.

Since Dad had cooked for the horse, and Gram was still out searching for Sweetheart, it was only fair that Sam made breakfast. She watched Dad walk out to the road to get the Sunday paper. Letting the door slam behind her, Sam hurried to the kitchen and rubbed her hands together. Even if it didn't measure up to Gram's cooking, Sam knew she could have a meal ready when he returned.

She used packaged biscuit mix instead of measuring flour and baking powder, but the biscuits were already baking as she heated a skillet and broke two eggs into its center. Sam hummed and the eggs sputtered. She was well on her way to making fried eggs just the way Dad liked them, until she reached the flipping-over part. She ended up serving them scrambled, but Dad didn't seem to notice.

"Good job, Sam," he said, from behind the newspaper.

Yawning with satisfaction, Sam was just loading strawberry jam onto a biscuit when Dad gave a long whistle of amazement.

His eyes were on the Darton newspaper as he folded back pages to show her a large advertisement.

Sam put the biscuit down and stared. Slocum had gone one step further in his campaign against the Phantom.

"Is this advertisement the same as the posters you and Jake told me about?" Dad tapped the sketch of the Phantom.

Sam nodded. Exactly the same, except she'd bet the Darton paper went to hundreds, maybe a thousand subscribers.

"This just won't do." Dad sat back, frowning. "The range is gonna be crawling with bounty hunters trying to lasso every mustang out there."

Sam decided the time was right to mention her plan.

"We should hop in the truck and get a head start," Sam said. "Jake and I discussed it yesterday. He's a great tracker, I've got pretty good horse sense and—" Sam checked Dad's expression and saw he wasn't going along with her. "At least that's what you said, didn't you—that I had good horse sense?"

"Pretty good," Dad said. "But, Sam, it's flat illegal."

"Only the mustang part," Sam contradicted him, then hurried to agree. "Probably BLM should know about this."

"Probably they already do," Dad said.

"Just in case they don't, I thought I'd call Miss Olson, Monday, as soon as the BLM office opens."

"Why wait?" Dad surprised Sam by opening a drawer and extracting a business card with a phone number inked on the back. A question flickered across Sam's mind. Why did Dad have Brynna's home telephone number? Was he considering the wild horse wrangler's job after all? The answer didn't matter today and, as it turned out, neither did having the number.

All day long, Brynna Olson's telephone rang and rang, but no one answered.

Sam could remember one other time she'd seen Gram this cranky. That time, she'd been worried over Sam. This time, she feared for Sweetheart. Gram had found no sign of the horses, and she didn't want to discuss her search. Instead, she instructed Sam to clean up the kitchen, do her outside chores, fold laundry, and finish her homework before riding with Jen.

Complaining would soak up valuable minutes, so Sam didn't do it. Even more than she wanted to meet Jen, Sam longed to reach War Drum Flats. Because it was visible from the highway, the flats were an unlikely place for Hammer to keep his mares. Still, the pond provided fresh water and she'd seen him there before, challenging the Phantom.

At last, she had permission to go, but Dad talked her out of riding Ace.

"If you kept him to a walk, there'd be no problem." Dad pointed out a swollen muscle under Ace's sleek hide. "But you'll want to gallop."

Sam agreed, and even though Ace neighed his jealousy, Sam saddled Strawberry.

"It's for your own good," Sam called to Ace.

She was telling Ace the truth. The change in mounts made her nervous. Though she'd ridden almost every day since she'd returned from San Francisco, Sam still doubted her ability. That accident, two years ago, had shaken her confidence.

Not that Sam questioned her skill at understanding horses. Each flicker of ears, each sidelong glance or movement of lips told her something. And Ace *had* helped her regain trust in her riding, but the fear of falling, far out on the empty plain, never left her. It was a secret she'd told no one.

Reins gripped tightly, Sam prepared to mount Strawberry. The mare stood just over fifteen hands tall. Now that Sam had brushed her, the mare looked almost pink.

Sam reminded herself how well she and Strawberry had done during the cattle drive, the day she'd let Ace rest by walking the trail riderless with the remuda.

Since fear telegraphed right down the reins to the horse's mouth, Sam told herself she wasn't afraid. She swung into the saddle and turned Strawberry toward the bridge.

"Be back before dark," Dad called, and Sam was off.

Pine-spiced wind blew down from the ridge and across War Drum Flats.

Strawberry moved with stiff, tight steps, but Sam couldn't tell why. A few sagebrush trembled as the wind blew past, but that shouldn't spook the mare. No mustangs clustered at the pond. More disappointing, no silver stallion stood guard on the ridge. Strawberry pulled at the bit, indicating she wanted to stop and drink from the pond. The pond's bank was muddy and marked with hoofprints. Apparently a few days of sunshine hadn't been enough to bake it hard after the storm.

Sam scanned the landscape all around. She didn't want to dismount, stand on the slick bank, and let Strawberry drink. She also didn't want to ride to the water's edge and lose contact with the mare's mouth while Strawberry leaned down to drink.

What was making her edgy? A breeze moaned through the wind-twisted pines up on the ridge. Somewhere up there lay Lost Canyon.

In childhood stories, she'd heard that this pond was the site of one of the last Indian battles. She couldn't recall details, but she thought Indians had swept down on cavalrymen as they watered their horses. The soldiers had been left afoot. The horses had been stolen and herded into Lost Canyon.

It was probably a myth. She could ask Jake about it, but he claimed not to care about his Native American heritage. Sam knew she'd have more luck asking his mom.

Anyway, nothing about the old story should make her nervous.

Strawberry sidestepped, stretched her neck toward the water, and gave a low whicker, asking how Sam could be so cruel.

"Oh all right, girl." Still mounted, Sam let the mare walk into the water. "Jen should be along in a minute, anyway."

Strawberry had taken two loud swallows when her head flew up. Too late, Sam tightened her grip on the reins.

On the ridge above them stood Hammer and Sweetheart. He sampled the wind, searching for the scent of a stallion that might interfere with his plan. His mane flapped as his head bobbed in satisfaction, and then he was running.

Hammer stampeded down the trail, nipping at Sweetheart's heels as they came. By the time she saw what had frightened Strawberry, Sam was falling.

Sam grabbed at Strawberry's mane as the mare lunged toward the other horses. Strawberry was drawn by the sight of Sweetheart, her pasture buddy, and put off by the bold stallion. Sam couldn't predict Strawberry's movements from one second to the next.

Sam had almost regained her seat when Strawberry slipped, clamored upright, then made for open ground. The mare's serpentine gallop kept Sam from settling into the saddle. She sagged to the right.

Suddenly, Strawberry gave a seesawing buck, then another.

Sam grabbed for the horn, but it wasn't enough. She wouldn't be able to ride this out, especially if Hammer moved in close. Sam's brain flashed a quick picture of arriving home on foot. Gram would forbid her to ride alone. Dad would shake his head in disappointment. Jake would treat her like a delicate girl.

Strawberry shambled to a stop, head turned in curiosity, then bolted a step.

Sam's head snapped back on her neck, but she refused to surrender Strawberry to Hammer. It was time to act, but she didn't know the right thing to do.

An experienced cowgirl would stay in the saddle, but if Strawberry bolted again, Sam knew she'd fall. Instead, Sam slid down Strawberry's left side, keeping her body pressed close to the mare, gripping the reins. Once her feet hit the dirt, Sam gave a quick jerk on the reins. The mare wheeled around to face

her and Sam felt a pulse of hope. She had Strawberry's attention.

"You're not going anywhere," she told the mare,
as the heavy-headed stallion approached.

Hammer left Sweetheart drinking from the pond.
Some distance away, two other mares waited.
Hotspot and an aged bay, whose head hung low, as if
she were winded, made up the rest of Hammer's
harem.

Neck arched, forelock tangled over his eyes,
Hammer came at them, set on increasing his band.

"Back off," Sam shouted, but he was a wild thing,
unafraid of human threats.

His skin shivered. Her noise irritated him.
Nothing more.

Strawberry lunged. Sam had wrapped the reins
around her hands. She held on, even when the small
bones in her hand grated together. A muscle binding
her arm to her shoulder stretched.

Oh no. She must hang on, no matter what, but if
her arm was pulled from her shoulder socket, her
determination would count for nothing.

Hammer came on. From the ground, his chest
looked broad as the front of a car. She was all that
stood between him and Strawberry. If he knocked
her out of the way, his heavy hooves would trample
her and he would take what he wanted.

If she waved her arms, he'd shy. But she couldn't
take a hand from the reins. Strawberry was already

dragging her around like a toy on a string. If Sam loosed her grip, the mare would be lost.

Strawberry dodged behind Sam, and Hammer's attitude changed. His ears flattened. His head lowered, swinging side to side, flinging froth on the dry desert floor.

"Get back!" she shouted, but the blue stallion came on.

He'd decided she was the enemy.

Chapter Thirteen ♋

ᚠOR AN INSTANT, Sam believed the thunder of hooves came from Strawberry. But the sound was all wrong and the pull to look back was irresistible.

The Phantom galloped to Sam's rescue. Head high, mane floating like white flame, he carved a half circle around her. With the whirlwind of his passing, Sam knew the Phantom had marked her as his. The explanation was hard to believe, but it was the only idea that made sense.

He'd come running from the ridge before, blocking Hammer from stealing a single mare. This time, none of his mares were here. Only Sam.

In Hammer's eagerness to steal Strawberry, he'd forgotten to be watchful. His stride shortened at the sight of the other stallion. As he veered away from Sam, the Phantom flew after him.

Sam hoped the fight would end as it had before. The Phantom pursued Hammer, nipping and slashing, herding the younger stallion away.

At first he went.

Proud of himself, the Phantom turned his back on Hammer. He settled into a fluid, carefree trot as he came back toward Sam.

She couldn't banish the fear she'd felt looking into Hammer's eyes. The Phantom was faster, more experienced, and probably smarter, but Hammer was thicker, desperate for a band of his own. His neck had never known the touch of a girl's hand. To the blue stallion, gentleness meant weakness.

The Phantom trotted closer to Sam. His ears twitched at the sound of her voice.

"Don't underestimate him," she muttered to the silver stallion. "Be ready, boy."

Maybe Hammer couldn't bear the memory of his other humiliation. His hooves sprayed earth as he swung back with the agility of a cutting horse.

The blue roan stopped long enough to scream a challenge. He held a grudge against the silver stallion, and this time he wouldn't run.

The Phantom wheeled around to face him.

Sam held her breath. The mares turned as still as horses carved of stone. No birds warbled. The wind stopped.

Sam wanted to throw rocks. She wanted to shout, to order her horse away from here. But the Phantom wasn't her horse anymore.

His neigh pierced the quiet, returning Hammer's

challenge. If the blue wanted a fight to the death, the Phantom would give it to him.

As if guided by knights carrying lances, the stallions trotted forward. Their strides lengthened, flowing into a lope, a gallop, then all grace fell away.

The stallions slammed together. In that first contact, they grappled to bite, to rip, to raise battering forelegs.

Sam backed off, towing Strawberry away from the sounds and lunging bodies. Speed was the Phantom's favorite weapon. He broke free of Hammer's teeth, spun away, watched for an opening, then darted in to bite and retreat once more.

What Hammer lacked in speed, he made up in weight. His massive shoulder clipped the Phantom's. His muscled haunches launched deadly kicks.

The two horses twisted in a haze of dust. Blood streaked their necks. Sweat marked them in dark swathes. Rage deepened their short neighs.

Please let him win. Please, if it's a fight to the death, let my horse live.

Sam covered her lips, muffling sounds that might distract the Phantom. As she did, she realized she held only one of Strawberry's reins. The mare wasn't pulling, wasn't looking. Neither was Hotspot or the bay. Was this what wild mares did? Wait for the victor to take over?

Despite her efforts, Sam made a moan of distress, and the Phantom glanced her way. It was a terrible mistake.

Hammer launched himself onto the Phantom's hindquarters, and both stallions crashed down into a snapping tangle of sagebrush.

No, no!

Bleeding, Phantom fought free of the brush.

Hammer shook his head, dizzied by the fall.

Then, as if he'd been hoarding more strength, the Phantom attacked.

Ears pinned hard against his neck, he rushed in, sprinted away. The blue stallion returned each charge, but the Phantom kept Hammer spinning, first this way, then that. Hammer didn't get a second chance to crush the light-boned silver stallion.

At last, staggering with weariness, the blue made a final effort. Hammer swung his massive head, trying to slam it against Phantom's delicate face.

He missed, the Phantom leaped past, and the effort cost the blue everything. He fell to his knees, beaten.

Blood made jagged paths over the Phantom's silver hide as he trotted around the beaten mustang. Phantom blared a victorious neigh, but Sam saw a stiffness, not yet a limp, in his gait.

Would he kill Hammer? Sam bit her lip, thinking. She knew about the survival of the fittest. She knew if they were on some isolated wild horse island, it would be right for Hammer to die. The Phantom's foals would be faster, smarter, stronger.

But Nature wasn't the boss on this range.

Humans interfered with the wild scheme of things. Hammer's herd might have been scattered by helicopters or run to death by kids on motorcycles. Hammer's only crime was following his instinct to have mares of his own. He didn't deserve to die.

Hammer regained his feet. His ears flicked toward Hotspot and the old bay. Then, without a backward glance, he bolted to them. Sweetheart followed him.

The silver stallion trembled with tension. Should he pursue the challenger or guard the ones he'd protected?

Sam knew the answer. More fighting, even with a weakened enemy, could hurt her horse enough that another stallion might defy him and win.

She didn't expect the Phantom to understand why the battle must end. She only hoped he'd listen.

"Zanzibar," Sam whispered the horse's secret name.

The tired stallion didn't look at her, but a soft nicker rumbled from him.

"Sweet boy," she said. After the fury and violence, no one would think her words made sense. But no one else could hear.

Hammer led his mares up a trail and vanished.

The silver stallion breathed deeply, searching for Hammer's odor. When he could catch it no more, he turned to Sam.

She fought back a cough. Dust stirred by the

fighting horses still hung on the air, but she squinted through it, judging her horse.

He liked to hear her talk. It soothed him, reminded him of the bond they'd forged in the warm stalls and lush pastures of River Bend Ranch. So, Sam talked.

"Hey, boy," she said. "Yeah, I hear Strawberry behind me and I see you looking, twitching your pretty ears. I think she's had enough of stallions today."

Strawberry pulled, tugging Sam away from the Phantom, and Sam released the single rein. It was a risk, but she had to move closer to the stallion.

"There, good boy, good Zanzibar."

The Phantom's nostrils fluttered, sucking in her scent. Once he'd been tricked by a sweater bearing her smell. Slocum had stolen the sweater and used the familiar scent to soothe the stallion. But no one could use the secret name to fool him, because no other soul on earth knew it.

He scuffed forward. Used to the crisp clip of his hooves, Sam looked down. Crimson blood welled from his left rear fetlock. He favored it as he walked.

"Hey, boy, does your leg hurt?" Sam kept talking as the Phantom approached. She wanted to bend and examine the wound, but she'd have better luck staying still. "You wouldn't allow it, would you? You'd snort and tell me a big, strong mustang like you takes care of himself."

Sam's fingers moved, wanting to touch him, and

the stallion noticed. He braced for an instant, then realized he had nothing to fear. At last, she could feel the warmth of his battle-weary body radiating toward her. Sam lifted her hand.

The stallion nuzzled it. The velvet of his muzzle and the prickle of his whiskers made Sam's heart sing.

"There's my beauty, my Zanzibar."

Sam closed her eyes as the horse lifted his head and rested it on her shoulder.

The stallion's pulse beat in his throat, through her shirt, and Sam's heart kept time with his.

Magic. Sam wished time would stop. She would stand like this, wrapped in this haze of enchantment forever.

Together, they heard the clink of a shod hoof on rock.

She felt the weight of the Phantom's head lift. By the time her eyes opened, he'd moved off a dozen yards.

The gray snorted, staring across the flats. Sam followed his gaze, but she didn't see a thing.

When she looked back at the Phantom, no drowsiness showed in his eyes. No weariness marked his movements. In one long leap, he passed sage and piñon and glinting desert rocks. He took the hidden path up to the ridge, and then he vanished.

Sam's hands shook as she swung back into Strawberry's saddle. The rider on the horizon had to be Jen.

"Get a grip," Sam scolded herself, but the mare's ears swiveled to listen. "Not you, Strawberry. You're doing fine, but you can't breathe a word of this adventure to anyone, got it?"

Thank goodness Jen had been too distant to see the Phantom. Sam just couldn't explain. Not until she knew Jen a lot better.

As Jen rode closer, Sam could tell why the palomino was named Silk Stockings. Her body shone dark gold except for front socks that reached her knees and emphasized her gait, making her look as if she were dancing.

"Sorry I'm late," called Jen.

"No problem. I just got here," Sam said. "Your mare is beautiful."

"Don't flatter Silly. It goes straight to her empty head." Jen didn't stop the mare from rubbing her cheek against Sam's leg. "See?"

"I wouldn't call you Silly if you were mine." Sam laughed, petting the mare's neck.

"Oh yes, you would," Jen said. "If not the first time she bucked you off at the horror of seeing a grasshopper, then you would when she dislocated your arm, shying at a paint chip on a fence."

At the reminder of Strawberry jerking her around like a rag doll, Sam rubbed her shoulder. Carrying a backpack tomorrow would ache.

"That's not Ace, I bet," Jen said, eyes sweeping Sam's mount.

"No, this is Strawberry," she admitted. "Ace . . ." Sam paused, but there was no point in hiding this information. Dad would report it to Brynna Olson tomorrow. "Got a little banged up last night."

"What happened?" Jen asked. Behind her glasses, Jen's blue eyes were concerned.

"The renegade stallion struck again and took Sweetheart, Gram's mare. Ace tried to stop him."

"Oh wow. What did he—"

"He got a couple bites that didn't amount to much, but the stallion rammed him up into the corner of two fences and Ace hurt his chest."

"Poor guy," Jen said, rubbing her own breastbone, but Sam saw Jen's curiosity beyond her sympathy. "Did you see the stallion? Was it the Phantom?"

"I saw him, and it wasn't. It was a blue roan. He has draft blood for sure, and the Phantom looks like an Arab, you know?"

"Of course, I don't know," Jen snapped in exasperation. "For most of my life, I thought he was a ghost story. Now, all of a sudden, everybody's seeing him, blaming things on him and Linc Slocum thinks you're a witch who can snap her fingers and have him appear."

"Well, I'm not," Sam said. "Or I'd conjure up gold instead of wishing my dad could have gotten a loop on that blue stallion, so we'd be rich."

"I saw that ad, too. *I'm* dying for the money, but

my parents think Slocum will be arrested before anyone can cash in on his offer." Jen's head bobbed from side to side as she considered that possibility. "Which wouldn't be all bad, either."

Sam laughed. As the mares jogged along side by side, she decided she liked Jen's sense of humor.

"Do you think he'd believe me if I told him it wasn't the Phantom?" Sam asked.

"I'm no expert on Slocum psychology," Jen said, "but I think he'd say something like, 'You'd say anything to protect that stud.'"

Sam turned in the saddle. "Why—?"

"I heard him say something like that to my dad. Slocum is convinced the Phantom was yours."

Was he? Jen didn't ask, but the question vibrated in the air between them.

Although it felt like telling a secret, Sam said, "I had a colt who ran away—"

"Sam, everyone knows about your accident."

"Okay, well it might be my colt Blackie, all grown up."

"Slocum claims you were up at BLM's Willow Springs holding pens, just riding that stallion around"—Jen spun her hand in the air—"like a carousel pony."

Sam's bark of laughter scared both horses. "Riding him around?"

Jen's smile said she hadn't really believed the story.

"Wanna gallop?" she asked.

Sam barely had time to nod.

Jen's palomino burst into a rollicking gallop, and Strawberry followed as if she'd been waiting for this all day.

Chapter Fourteen ɕ

ℳONDAY MORNING, Darton High School was covered with campaign posters.

"I don't know why we don't do these elections in the spring, like other high schools," Jen grumbled as she and Sam entered the school. "Starting the year with a popularity contest doesn't seem like a good idea."

"On the other hand," Sam said, nudging her friend with an elbow, "you're a freshman, so what do you know?"

"How do I keep forgetting?" Jen asked, pretending to strike her forehead in frustration. She turned left toward her locker. "See you in gym."

"Bye." Sam scanned the campaign posters as she walked to her own locker. The posters were much the same as those in her San Francisco middle school.

The candidates' appeals were painted on construction paper or butcher paper, sometimes decorated with glitter or clever slogans.

Sam had almost reached her locker when a swarm of students blocked her way. They stared at something on the wall.

Rachel Slocum's campaign poster was different.

Five minutes before the first class of the week, Rachel was already drawing a crowd. The banner looked like a glossy magazine page featuring four full-color photographs of Rachel. Though the poster was big as a double bed, Sam had to jostle through the crowd to see.

Rachel as treasurer . . . will root for you promised hot-pink script across a cheerleader-skirted Rachel leaping in the air. *Rachel as treasurer . . . will shine for you* said letters across homecoming queen Rachel, hair spilling in a coffee-brown waterfall down her back. *Rachel as treasurer . . . will work for you* showed her bent over a notebook, wearing glasses and a flattering little frown. The last picture, a computer-generated composite of real Rachel and towering stacks of cartooned gold coins and dollar bills, had students chuckling and pointing. *Rachel as treasurer will save every dime for you* it pledged.

"She'd know about money, all right," a lanky boy said with grudging admiration.

The first bell shattered Sam's contemplation. She sprinted for her locker, dialed her combination, and tried to review her history homework. There was no reason to waste brain time on Rachel. But Sam would bet Rachel had recovered from her convenient Friday illness and those expensive posters were the price Linc Slocum had paid for embarrassing his little princess.

Gym class was an all-grades torture session. Freshman had lockers next to juniors. Sophomores averted their eyes when they showered with seniors. Only luck gave Sam and Jen P.E. lockers in the same row.

Now, they gossiped as they dressed for a one-mile jog followed by flag football.

"The ranch was her mom's dream," Jen whispered as she pulled on green shorts. "Slocum just went along, at first. Then he got hooked by the"— Jen paused and a sly smile claimed her face— "charm of the Old West."

Sam glanced all around before she asked, "So, where's the mom now? England? Really?"

"She remarried, a baron or something, and lives on a horse farm outside Nottingham."

"Wow." Sam gave a final tug to her tennis shoe laces. "So, when Rachel's there, do you suppose she has tea with the Queen?"

Jen sputtered with laughter. "You're turning evil, Sam. I don't think I'm a good influence on you."

The locker-room crowd had thinned by the time they bolted toward the athletic field.

Rachel Slocum stood, framed in the doorway, waiting for them. Outside, Sam saw girls jogging around the track, ponytails bouncing, but Rachel didn't seem to care if she was late.

"If you keep gossiping about my dad, or do anything to damage my campaign," Rachel said, "you'll be a social outcast this fast." Rachel snapped her fingers beneath Sam's nose.

Sam felt a hot blush claim her face. Last week, she'd been the only one in school *not* spreading rumors about Linc Slocum.

Very slowly, Sam tucked a lock of auburn hair behind one ear. She wasn't feeling scared, she realized, just surprised by Rachel's ambush.

"I'm not gossiping about your dad," Sam said.

Rachel fluttered her rose-gold fingernails just inches from Sam's cheek, as if shooing her away.

"In fact," Sam pressed on, "I'm kind of insulted you think I have nothing better to do than spend time thinking about your dad. If he didn't keep showing up where I was, I wouldn't even know him."

"It's that horse." Rachel shuddered. "He's no different from all the others, I'm sure. They're all dirty, smelly, and big enough to hurt you but so stupid they don't realize it. If they had an ounce of intelligence, they'd realize they don't have to carry people around on their filthy backs."

"This horse is wild, Rachel," Jen interrupted.

"So? This time my father's obsessed with a wild horse. Before that it was spotted horses. Who cares? It's his hobby."

Outside, a whistle shrilled as the teacher called the girls together.

"Excuse me," Sam said, slipping past Rachel.

"There are *no* excuses for you, cowgirl," Rachel snapped. "Just remember that."

During lunch, Rachel's campaign drew even more attention. Instead of handing out paper badges or campaign buttons, Rachel passed out dollar bills. Stamped across George Washington's face in hot-pink ink were the words *Rachel for Treasurer*.

Sam and Jen heard talk of the tactic, but Sam didn't see it with her own eyes until she filed into journalism class and Daisy handed her a dollar.

"Rachel would just love to have your vote," Daisy gushed.

Don't react. Sam told herself. *Don't sneer or fling it back in her face.*

She managed to appear calm, but Sam couldn't stop herself from thinking of Dad's disappointment over the few cents per pound they hadn't made on the cattle.

She kept her feet moving away from Daisy, but Sam still pictured Gram brooding over each new batch of bills.

Sam had almost reached her desk when Rachel squirmed into her path.

"Here, cowgirl." Rachel pressed another dollar into Sam's hand. "You look like you could use an extra."

"Rachel, I'm pretty sure this is illegal." RJay's bellow was so well-timed, Sam wondered if the student editor had overheard Rachel's insult. "From what I've heard," he said, examining one of the bills, "you're not going to like prison."

Rachel's fingers went gliding through her hair as she gave a theatrical sigh. "As long as they have MTV and a decent manicurist, I'll manage."

Sam didn't want to laugh, but she did. Was it possible a decent human being lurked beneath that catty exterior? Probably not.

She forgot about Rachel during the quiz on the weekend's homework. Her fingers were aching from writing fast, when Mr. Blair called time.

"Pass 'em up and listen," Mr. Blair yelled above the complaints of those who hadn't studied for the quiz. He put the papers aside and crossed his arms. "As students from last year know, we've got three cameras for staff use. Nikons donated by the Darton *Review-Journal*. Donated," Mr. Blair emphasized, "but very expensive to replace.

"Since last year's staff only produced one decent photographer and he's now editor in chief—" Mr. Blair paused as RJay bowed to nonexistent applause "—I'll let new students try out as photographers."

Excitement rushed through Sam's veins.

"If you're interested, check one out overnight, shoot one roll of film, then submit it to me and RJay. Impress us," Mr. Blair hollered, "because we will decide whose work earns the right to keep the camera for the first semester."

Murmurs rustled as students turned to each other, but Sam didn't talk. She focused on the plan forming in her imagination.

"Class? One more thing. You'll treat these cameras like delicate baby birds. Do not harm them in any way. Got that?

"If they break, I won't care whose fault it is." Mr. Blair paced the front of the classroom, pointing at students during his tirade. "If *your* mama breaks it or *your* dog eats it or *you*, Miss Forster, get abducted by aliens—*you* pay the five hundred dollars to replace the camera."

Sam smiled at her journalism teacher. It didn't matter that Mr. Blair had singled her out. Her idea was bubbling like a shaken soda—sweet and ready to explode.

Mr. Blair's glare swept the entire class. "You break it, you buy it. No excuses."

Sam's nerves hummed with excitement. She'd be careful, all right, because one of those black and silver cameras would help her earn that reward money and prove to Linc Slocum the Phantom was not to blame.

Shooting the test roll of film wasn't easy. She took a few shots at school, but she was afraid they wouldn't turn out. Only after Sam got the camera, did she realize photography wasn't a simple point-and-shoot operation. There were shutter speeds to consider and focus to figure out.

Sam was growling with frustration by the time she really listened to Gram's suggestion.

"Just call Maxine," Gram said. "Maxine Ely is a talented photographer. Her work wins blue ribbons at the state fair and the Darton library has framed prints of her pictures hanging on the walls."

Sam bit her lip, listening, but too sheepish to do anything.

"She's Jake's mother, for heaven's sake, not just your history teacher," Gram said. "She's known you since you were in diapers."

"That doesn't make it better, Gram."

But Sam's determination to get the reward from Slocum won out over her fretting.

Sam called.

Three times. Each time, Mrs. Ely acted as if helping Sam was the highlight of her day. *She must really like photography*, Sam thought.

And it was sort of exciting. Sam jogged from place to place on the ranch. She took a picture of Buddy trying to scratch her nose with a rear hoof, and one of a rusty hinge that had always looked too fancy for the gate. She gave up trying to make a portrait of Ace. The gelding was so friendly and curious, he kept nuzzling the lens.

"You are too cute for your own good," Sam said.

She kissed his tender muzzle, then jogged toward the River Bend bridge, imagining the last picture she'd take before darkness fell.

Sam's last thoughts as she fell asleep were, as always, of the Phantom. In the sparkling mist of a dream, he ran toward her, ears cupped to hear her voice, dark eyes soft and filled with her face.

Oh no. Sam sat up. She'd forgotten to call Brynna Olson.

How stupid was she? Sam buried both hands in her short hair and pulled. *Idiot.* Nothing was more important than protecting him.

Dad had gone to bed an hour ago. Sam listened intently. Was that the clink of a spoon on pottery? Hadn't Gram said she might stir up a batch of sourdough bread and let it rise in the refrigerator overnight?

Sam pattered down the stairs so fast, she was actually breathless when she came into the kitchen.

"Did Dad call Brynna about Slocum's posters and that ad?"

Gram nodded. She pulled plastic wrap over the top of the bowl, then did it again, tighter.

Sam nearly shouted in frustration until it hit her. This wasn't going to be good news.

"What?" Sam croaked.

"Brynna left Sunday for Washington. She'll be gone at least a week." Gram paused to let that news

sink in. "Wyatt spoke to her replacement, a gentle-
man from the BLM office in Las Vegas."

Las Vegas? Sam's mind spun with flashes of neon
lights and tuxedoed gamblers. She'd never been to
Las Vegas. What she was thinking was probably
unfair, because she was thinking Brynna's replacement couldn't possibly understand wild horses.

"What did he say?" Sam heard her voice croak.

Gram sighed, closed the refrigerator, then leaned
against it. "He said it was 'bothersome,' but he was
sure it was a difficulty that would blow over without
his interference."

Sam couldn't sleep. She resented the night,
because she had to move fast.

Without Brynna's help, her plan might be the
only thing between the Phantom and capture. She
tossed and turned all night, picturing the stallion's
injured fetlock. If it made him slow, some cowboy
could lasso him.

She dreamed of Flick, the cowboy with the
drooping handlebar mustache. He'd worked at
Slocum's Gold Dust Ranch before his temporary
position at the Willow Springs Wild Horse Center.
While working for the BLM, Flick had illegally
roped the Phantom and Brynna had fired him. Flick
had disappeared after that, but Slocum would know
where to find him. Sam was sure of it.

◖◗

The next morning before classes began, Sam tracked down Mr. Blair and handed him the camera and the film.

"Overachiever, huh, Forster?" he asked.

"I guess so," she answered, but she could tell his gruff question had been a compliment.

Mrs. Ely pulled her aside after history and made her promise to stop by after school and show her the pictures.

"I don't think Mr. Blair will have had time to develop them," Sam said. "And I can't miss the bus after school."

"Mr. Blair might surprise you. He's in the school darkroom as much as he's in class. And after school—"

Mrs. Ely glanced over Sam's shoulder for a second. Sam turned, too, and saw Rachel pretending to gather her books, though she was clearly eavesdropping.

"—I can always give you a ride home," Mrs. Ely continued, "if you miss your bus."

"Thanks. I'll bring them, if I can," Sam said.

Her spirits soared as she hurried to her next class, even though Rachel pushed past her with a sour expression. Rachel always looked that way in history. After all, she was a sophomore taking a freshman class. She must have flunked last year.

Sam had just swallowed the last of her peanut butter sandwich and walked toward the journalism classroom, when she saw Mr. Blair, waiting outside the door. Sam's heart plummeted and she had to force her fingers out of the fists they had curled into.

What stupid thing had she done? Left the lens cap on so that the entire roll of pictures turned out blank? Broken some mechanism she hadn't even noticed?

Her steps must have slowed, because Mr. Blair shouted down the hall. "Too late now, Forster." His voice caused a dozen heads to turn and stare. "Come in and face the music."

Mr. Blair had used the school darkroom to develop and print the photographs that were now spread over a table in the back of the room. Those who'd arrived early were already looking at them, and Mr. Blair didn't make them leave as he gave Sam an evaluation of her work.

"This one shows evidence of nearly every mistake a beginner can make." Mr. Blair tapped a picture Sam had taken of a reflection on a watering trough. "This is better, but you've got to read up on lens openings and shutter speeds." His finger skimmed above a photograph of two Herefords at dusk.

"Your people pictures are the best," RJay said as he scooted one photo away from the others.

Sam bit her lip in surprise. It was one of the after-school shots she'd taken before her telephone tutoring from Mrs. Ely. She'd lucked out on this one.

In it, Ms. Santos was tapping at her computer keyboard with one hand, a telephone clamped between her ear and shoulder, smiling and beckoning a student into her office.

"We'll use this for the next issue," RJay said, and Mr. Blair nodded.

She felt dizzy, as if she hovered above the whole scene. Other students studied the photos and gave her sidelong glances that could have been admiration or amazement that she'd done something noteworthy.

Maybe she had, and maybe it could help her save the Phantom.

And then Mr. Blair held up the one photograph she'd wanted to erase as soon as she'd snapped it.

In it, Rachel stood by one of her campaign posters. Her forced toothpaste-commercial smile looked just like her dad's. One hand was perched on her hip and the other hand flicked out, the light caught on her glittering fingernails as she made a point to a bedraggled-looking freshman boy.

"This one is priceless," Mr. Blair said.

Laughter sparked all around her, but Sam only felt the hot stare of Rachel's eyes on the nape of her neck.

RJay took the photograph from Mr. Blair and pretended to make up a caption for it. "'In honor of my campaign, dahling, I'm wearing my new fuchsia-periwinkle nail enamel. So very chic, don't you know.'"

For a minute, Sam felt sick, but when she finally risked a look, Rachel was smiling. She was a better sport than Sam would have thought.

"I think, Miss Forster, you should take the camera for another night and see if you can refine your touch with lighting," Mr. Blair said. "Come back at the end of the day to pick it up."

When the last bell rang, Sam jumped from her seat and got to Mr. Blair's classroom as quickly as she could. She didn't have much time to get the camera and make it to the bus on time.

Mr. Blair was waiting for her at his desk.

"Try playing with the aperture," he told her, "to alter your depth of field."

Sam glanced at the classroom clock. Jen would be saving her a seat on the bus. If she talked fast, she might have time to ask a few questions.

Mr. Blair answered every question, then paused.

"You seem awfully interested in shooting in low-light situations," Mr. Blair said.

Carefully Sam looped the camera strap over her neck.

"I am, sort of," she admitted. Sam checked the clock and saw she had no time for half-true explanations.

She couldn't tell anyone about her plan to take pictures of the thieving blue roan.

"Thanks for the help," Sam said and hurried away.

With the camera around her neck, she didn't dare

run, but the smell of diesel fumes from the idling buses made her walk in long strides.

Sam would have made it to the bus, if Mrs. Ely hadn't leaned from her classroom door.

"Come tell me," she said.

Sam couldn't resist telling Mrs. Ely how much her advice had helped.

"He loved them," Sam said. "Well, except—"

A desk moved in the front row of the empty classroom. What was Rachel doing here again?

Mrs. Ely followed Sam's glance. "Rachel thinks a pen might have rolled out of her backpack during class, so she's searching for it."

Bent to look under a desk, Rachel flashed a lopsided grin.

"Got it," Rachel said, but she didn't leave.

"So, you're in a hurry and don't have the photographs with you," Mrs. Ely summed up the situation. "I'll let you run, but first there's a photography book you should have. I want you to borrow my copy, but it's up there." Mrs. Ely rushed across the classroom to a soaring bookcase crammed with books. She pointed to the top shelf. "I think you can reach it better than I can."

Sam smiled. It was funny being taller than her teacher. It would only take a minute.

"Okay," she said. Carefully, Sam removed the camera from around her neck. She looked around for a place to put it. Mrs. Ely's desk was sort of a mess.

"I'll hold it for you," Rachel offered.

Sam's hands tightened on the camera. She told herself her paranoia was just plain childish. She handed the camera to Rachel and went to stand beside her teacher.

"It is kind of high," she said, standing on tiptoe.

Sam's index finger locked on the book's spine, and it plummeted to the floor. An apology was forming on Sam's lips when she heard the sound.

Metal slammed against tile. A fraction of a second later, there came the tinkling of glass.

Without meaning to, Sam covered her ears. She didn't have to turn around to identify the sound. She'd just heard the shattering of her dreams.

Chapter Fifteen ❧

"SAMANTHA, OH MY gosh." Rachel's hands covered her mouth in mock horror. "There must have been something slippery on it. That camera just slid right through my hands."

Rachel's eyes showed no sympathy as she looked at Sam and shrugged. "Wow, you know what Mr. Blair said. Those cameras cost five hundred dollars and if it's checked out to you, it's your problem. No matter what."

Mrs. Ely had already picked up the camera. She turned it carefully, looking through the viewfinder.

"Ta-ta until tomorrow," Rachel chirped, and her perfume lingered in the room like a taunt.

Rachel had broken the camera. Sam knew it, and by her jerky movements, Mrs. Ely knew it, too. But their certainty wouldn't matter to Mr. Blair. *You break it, you buy it. No excuses.*

This is what it feels like to be in shock, Sam thought.

She took the camera from Mrs. Ely and wandered down the empty hall.

No buses remained outside Darton High School. The only moving vehicle was Rachel's baby-blue Mercedes-Benz.

Sam stood there, priming herself to refuse Rachel's offer of a ride home. She had dropped the camera on purpose. It would feel good to refuse to even be in the same car with her.

When Rachel drove off without a backward look, Sam felt her backpack's weight would drag her to her knees. She could call Gram or Dad to come get her, but then she'd have to tell them about the camera even sooner.

A sigh lifted her chest and gusted out How could she pay for the camera? She loved her life at River Bend, but there were no luxuries to give up.

In a single swoop, Rachel had robbed her of Mr. Blair's respect, Gram and Dad's approval, the Phantom's rescue, and money. Lots of money.

"I suppose those useless sons of mine are long gone." Mrs. Ely was suddenly beside Sam. Mrs. Ely wore fresh red lipstick and her blond curls bounced as she scanned the parking lot and jingled her car keys. "They're more fun, but I have a nicer car."

Sam stared at Mrs. Ely, knowing she should say something.

"Come with me," the teacher said, and beckoned Sam toward a green sedan.

Sam felt boneless, but she managed to climb in and fasten her seat belt. As they drove, Mrs. Ely talked about school. She described an upcoming history project she hoped would be fun. When Sam only nodded, Mrs. Ely gave up conversation in favor of the radio news. After a few minutes, she snapped off the radio.

"Can we pretend I'm not your teacher?" she asked.

"What?" Sam shook her head in confusion.

Mrs. Ely kept her eyes on the road, but she extended her right hand toward Sam. "Glad to meet you. I'm your neighbor Maxine. Jake's mommy. Our cows sure are loving that alfalfa we got from Wyatt."

Sam laughed. The out-of-order sign on her brain could be removed. Suddenly, she understood Mrs. Ely wanted to say something un-teacherly. Sam hoped it was something vile about Rachel.

"Do you think it was an accident?" Mrs. Ely asked.

"Maybe," Sam said. "I wasn't looking."

"It looks like the mirror is broken. That was the tinkling sound, but I didn't want to take it apart and check. That's work for an expert."

Sam felt her scalp tighten against her skull. Experts were always expensive.

"If Rachel broke it, she should pay for it."

When Sam explained what Mr. Blair had told the class, Mrs. Ely's expression darkened.

"That could be sticky, since he took a stand in front of the class," Mrs. Ely admitted. "Still, if I told him the truth . . ."

Mrs. Ely's voice trailed off. Neither of them had *seen* Rachel do it.

"Mr. Blair said we were responsible, no matter whose fault it was," Sam repeated.

They drove in silence a while longer, but Sam suspected Mrs. Ely was having a serious talk with herself. She frowned, then nodded, raised one blond eyebrow, then her frown vanished.

"So, what is it you're yearning to photograph?" Mrs. Ely asked. "You wouldn't be shy if you knew what I like to shoot best."

"Your family?" Sam guessed.

"Sometimes, but it's tough to catch them being themselves. Those men of mine work hard at being stoic." Mrs. Ely lowered the car windows to let the late August breezes surround them. "No, I like to photograph windows. Windows that reflect faces or mountains, windows that let you see inside to a family dinner table—" She shrugged. "Just windows. Nothing could be artier than that."

"Wild horses," Sam admitted. "At night."

The invading breeze ruffled the ungraded papers Mrs. Ely had tossed in the backseat. Sam noticed a flash of yellow on the road, ahead. They'd catch the school bus soon.

"Oh, Sam," Mrs. Ely said, staring ahead. "What

an incredible idea. I wonder," she mused, "what kind of equipment you'd need to do it right."

"Well," Sam said as they drew alongside the bus, "a camera would be a start."

Sam saw Jen. Sam leaned forward. She waved, trying to catch Jen's eye. Once she did, Jen looked puzzled, then angry.

Oh no. Sam just knew Jen was thinking she'd stood her up.

Sure enough, Jen straightened, pressed her shoulders against the seat back, and turned away.

Oh great, Sam thought. *This day just keeps getting better and better.*

When it seemed nothing else could go wrong, they arrived at River Bend. Mrs. Ely switched off the engine, said, "Be right back," then hurried to tell Dad what had happened.

Surprised and horrified, Sam froze next to Mrs. Ely's car.

Near the barn, Dallas and Ross were conspiring with Dad to shoe Tank, Ross's bald-faced bay. Dad hated shoeing horses in general and Tank in particular. It took two men to hold Tank while a third wielded the hammer and horseshoe nails.

Mrs. Ely crossed the ranch yard in her tidy slacks and blazer, then folded her arms and stood talking.

From here, Sam couldn't tell if Dad had finished shoeing Tank before he laid the hammer on the ground and walked away. Each step was firm and deliberate, but Mrs. Ely followed him. Sam wondered if Jake's mom was doing more harm than good.

She didn't have to wonder long. Mrs. Ely came storming back, shaking her head.

"Never marry a cowboy, Samantha," Mrs. Ely said. She leaned against the car next to Sam and stared toward the Calico Mountains. "Pride is their downfall, and that's for sure."

"Am I grounded until I'm eighteen?"

"No." Mrs. Ely looked over at her suddenly. "Oh, Samantha, of course not. You're not in trouble. I just suggested Wyatt make a private arrangement with Slocum, to cover his daughter's carelessness. You'd think I suggested something illegal."

Sam felt relieved she wasn't in trouble but not surprised at Dad's reaction. "Yeah, Dad's like that."

"Aren't they all." Mrs. Ely rubbed her hands together. "The men of Three Ponies Ranch are exactly the same as those at River Bend."

Mrs. Ely took the camera from Sam and looked at it once more. "Well, maybe the repair won't be too expensive. Until it's fixed, though, the least I can do is lend you a camera."

"It wasn't your fault," Sam protested, taking the Nikon back.

"She heard me ask you to come in after school. Then, she arranged to be there, too." Mrs. Ely's red lips pressed together, but she just couldn't stay silent.

"Of course, I'm not suggesting Rachel would do something destructive because you're getting lots of attention from your teachers and classmates. What kind of teacher would even hint at such a thing?"

"Not you," Sam said.

"Not me. I'm glad we've got that straight," Maxine Ely blurted, but she was laughing as she climbed back into her car. "Jake'll be over with that camera. Soon."

The phone was ringing when Sam walked into the white ranch house.

"It's Jennifer Kenworthy." Gram extended the telephone receiver toward Sam, then whispered, "She doesn't sound very happy."

"Hello?" Sam let her backpack down to the floor.

"So, you got a better offer and ditched me?" Jen meant her tone to be sarcastic, but it sounded hurt. "Next time, let me know, so I don't feel dumb saving you a seat."

"I missed the bus." Sam tried to keep the weariness from her voice, but a glance from Gram said she wasn't doing a good job. "Because Rachel broke the camera Mr. Blair loaned me."

Jen gasped as if someone had poured cold water down her neck. "The Nikon?"

"The Nikon."

"I suppose Mrs. Ely was your escort home because the school police think you're a flight risk.

So, are you making a run for the border?"

"Jen, this isn't funny." Sam's mouth smiled in spite of her gloom.

"I know." Jen took a breath, then asked, "How much?"

"I don't know yet. It makes a tinkling sound when you shake it."

"That doesn't sound good," Jen said. After a few seconds silence, she asked, "How deep?"

Sam took a glass of lemonade from Gram and repeated, "How *deep*?"

"Yeah, how deep are we going to bury Rachel's body?"

"You are really awful." Sam wavered between laughing and crying. "But you're not still mad at me, right?"

"Not this time," Jen said. "Even though you probably want to put off our ride for a really interesting family discussion."

"Oh yeah," Sam said, looking at Gram's impatient expression. "Interesting."

Sam braced herself for further explanation, but as soon as she hung up the phone, it rang again. Because her voice was still unsteady, Sam let Gram answer.

"Hello," Gram said. "Oh, Maxine."

Sam lifted the cookie jar lid, quietly, so she could listen. She loaded three raisin-fat oatmeal cookies onto a saucer, then poured a glass of milk.

"Is that so?" Gram said. "A knack? He said 'promising' and that little—" Gram broke off. "Samantha, please take your snack upstairs and get started on your homework."

Sam trotted upstairs. At least Gram and Dad didn't seem mad at her. She could be grateful for that.

A shrill wind chased around the house, banging the shutters on Sam's window.

It was almost dinnertime, but she heard Jake pull up in his Dad's truck. As she folded away her biology worksheet and stacked her books, Sam could hear past the wind and knew Jake was talking to Dad and Gram.

When Sam came down the stairs, she could tell he'd laid out some sort of plan.

Jake wore a brick-colored shirt Sam hadn't seen before. It was tucked into faded jeans. The scuffed toes of his boots showed as he leaned against the kitchen door, but Jake smelled like soap and his black hair was shiny.

Something was up, and Sam felt uneasy.

"You want to drive down by War Drum Flats, lay low, and see if some stallion shows up with Sweetheart and that Appaloosa of Slocum's?" Jake asked.

Sam's glance flew to Dad, then Gram.

"I packed some sandwiches and a thermos of cocoa, so you can get there before dark." Gram indicated a brown paper bag. "If the lead mare sees you there as part of the scenery, she'll be less spooked than if you drive up later."

It made sense, but Sam wondered why Gram and Dad were going along with this scheme.

"But it's a school night," Sam blurted.

Jake groaned an instant before Dad spoke.

"That's right," Dad said. "You've got a watch and you'd better use it. I expect you in bed by ten o'clock."

"Yes, sir," Sam said.

Gram handed Sam the bag and kissed her cheek. "See if you can find Sweetheart for me, dear."

"Okay, Gram."

Jake opened the door, lifted her sheepskin coat from a hook, and shoved it toward her. Nights on the range could turn cold, even after ninety-degree days. Sam took it, then hurried, before Gram and Dad changed their minds.

"Don't ask me," Jake said, as Sam fell into step beside him. "It's Mom's doin' and I'm just your chaperone."

Sam's mind spun as they left the ranch, crossed the River Bend bridge, and headed into the wind toward War Drum Flats.

She hadn't told Maxine Ely the details of her plan, just that she wanted to photograph horses at night. Somehow, though, Maxine had figured it out and sent Jake to help.

Jake on a horse *might* help by roping Hammer, but this Jake—looking mature and in charge at the steering wheel—could just as easily get in her way.

Sam crossed her arms in determination.

"Your hair's okay," Jake said, without looking at her.

"What a relief," Sam said. "You can't imagine how many nights I've stayed awake worrying that—"

"Don't annoy the driver," Jake interrupted. "I just thought I'd mention I'm getting used to it." He switched on the truck's heater. "You should know, though, guys always think it's a mistake when girls cut their hair."

"I'll write it in my diary," Sam sneered, but they both relaxed after that.

As the sun dropped behind the mountains, the glow from the instrument panel made the truck's dark cab almost cozy.

"Remember when we were little and you used to tell me Indian stories?" Sam asked.

"I remember that you were a pest and I could bore you into falling asleep so you would leave me alone."

Sam shivered. "I was never bored," she said, pulling her sheepskin coat closer. It was a good thing she'd brought it, since the truck's heater barely did its job. "How many of those stories were true?"

"Lots of them are legends. People all over the country substitute the names of their own tribes or heroes. I don't know." Jake shrugged. "Mom could tell you better than I could."

When Jake still didn't offer a story, Sam began planning. "Can you park the truck off the road? Then I'll walk down by the water. Like Gram said, if I'm just sitting there—"

"We."

"What?" Sam felt a shimmer of irritation.

"If *we're* just sitting there, the horses are more likely to approach."

"Thanks, Jake, but you can stay in the nice warm truck. All I'm going to do is take a picture—"

"With *my mom's* camera, *if* I decide to give it to you."

"Don't be bratty, Jake."

"Try 'sensible,' Pest." Jake glanced into the rearview mirror, then pulled the truck off the street, onto a dirt road.

"Explain why it's more sensible for both of us to sit in the cold, waiting for mustangs that probably won't show up."

"If you scare them," Jake said patiently, "you could be hurt. Horses, you might've heard, are really big."

Sam folded her hands. He was so annoying, it was a challenge to stay calm.

"If the horses spooked, they'd run away from me. And if they accidentally ran my way, do you think you can single-handedly stop a stampede? If you can, so can I." Sam took a long breath, thinking of how she'd freed the Phantom from the Willow Springs corrals. "Sometimes, I don't mess up, Jake. Sometimes, I do things right."

Jake let her words hang there between them.

Sam didn't force him to reply. She just bounced against her seat belt as he guided the truck over the rutted road. It was five minutes before he slowed down.

"Let's eat before we go down there," Jake said. "My mom sent food, too."

As the truck stopped uphill from the pond, behind a screen of wind-tossed piñons, Sam let Jake believe he'd won. It would be good for his digestion.

Using the big purple first aid kit as a picnic table, they feasted on roast beef sandwiches, corn chips, and cocoa from Gram, and Swiss cheese on rye, carrot sticks, and bottled water from Jake's mother.

They chewed in such companionable silence, Sam was reluctant to rekindle their fight. She searched for words that weren't a declaration that she was, by golly, going out there alone.

The evening had turned midnight blue around them, but a smudge of tan showed against the eastern hills.

"Does that trail lead to Lost Canyon?" Sam asked.

Jake followed her pointing finger and nodded.

"Why's it called that, do you know?"

Jake narrowed his eyes, as if she were trying to trick him.

"What?" Sam demanded.

Jake settled back against the driver's door and rolled a bottle of water between his palms. "I'll only tell you this story because I'm too full to move."

"Oh, good." Sam leaned against her own door and nestled into her coat. She pulled the sheepskin collar against her cheeks, still watching the window behind him, in case mustangs appeared.

"A band of Shoshone—not a hunting party or families with tents, but warriors—holed up in Lost Canyon with their war ponies. Stories say they had a hundred of the West's fastest horses, and each night they led them down to water."

Jake pointed at the pond. "In those days, that was a huge lake, blue as a bowl full of sky, with water so pure and sweet the horses craved it more than grass.

"After the Civil War, cavalrymen stationed at the remount station by Alkali had little to do. Through the war, they'd captured mustangs, broken them to saddle, and sent them off to Southern battlefields.

"After the war, there was only Indian fighting, clearing Shoshones and Paiutes off this land for farmers.

"Hoofprints told the cavalrymen of the one hundred Shoshone ponies, and the soldiers set a trap. Why didn't the warriors see it?" Jake wondered. "Was it a foggy night? Were the horses thirstier than usual and less wary? No one knows."

Outside the truck, Sam heard an insect, but nothing else moved.

"Did they kill them?" she asked.

"They captured them and corralled the ponies. The horses could have made a run for it. They might have escaped, but herd instinct is stronger than anything. If a horse is left behind, he's prey to coyotes and cougars. Safety is with the herd. Usually."

Sam hugged her knees to her chest. She didn't want to hear the rest of the story, but she wouldn't make Jake stop.

"These soldiers were cavalrymen. They understood the superiority of a mounted warrior over a man on foot. So they took what the Shoshone valued more than life—their war ponies.

"The shooting started at dawn. It's said all the penned ponies screamed each time a rifle cracked and the next horse fell. By noon, the soldiers were sickened by the blood-slick ground and frightened by warriors chanting death songs. But their orders said to slaughter every pony and they did.

"They released the Shoshone. Why shouldn't they? The Indians' power lay stinking on the desert floor, dinner for vultures. With the cries of dying horses still echoing from the hills, the cavalrymen watched the Shoshone warriors walk the long trail to Lost Canyon."

Wind made the truck shudder and Sam rubbed her arms against a sudden chill. It was lucky she wasn't superstitious, Sam thought. A more fearful sort might mistake the wailing wind for the sound of ghost ponies, crying for their lost companions.

"Releasing the Shoshone was a mistake," Jake said. In the darkness, his teeth showed in a faint smile. "One man and three ponies had stayed behind. Three ponies is a small fighting force, for sure, but the warriors petted them and trained them. They decorated them in war paint with red prints on their shoulders and blue rings around their eyes. The warriors fasted, prayed, and vowed to wait.

"One day, a small cavalry patrol trotted across the desert, confident they could pass in safety. When they heard Shoshone drums, they laughed. What would the brave warriors do? Chase after them on foot?"

"But wait." Sam remembered. "The last Indian battle in Nevada was fought on War Drum Flats, right?"

"Not much of a battle." Jake's tone turned casual. "Not a single man died, but the Shoshone warriors took the horses and left the cavalrymen to walk back to the fort, proving the power of one man and three ponies."

"And that's how your ranch got its name," Sam said.

"I guess." Jake shrugged. "You ready to walk down there?"

He turned on the headlights to light their way.

Sam started to reply, then stopped. She blinked,

making sure the combination of moonlight and head-lights hadn't fooled her eyes.

"Behind you," she whispered.

For a second, Jake turned to stone, then smoothly and slowly his head swiveled to look out the window.

Down the trail from Lost Canyon came the Phantom's herd, without him.

Chapter Sixteen ❧

"I<small>T'S THE</small> P<small>HANTOM'S</small> herd, but where is he?"

In the darkness outside Jake's truck, Sam made out the lead mare with zebra-striped forelegs. She spotted one of the blood-bay mares, too, but the silver stallion was missing.

"Relax." Jake jiggled her arm in a way he must think was calming. "You're breathing too fast for someone just sitting in a truck."

"Jake, a couple days ago, the Phantom was in a fight. He won, but he was injured."

Cautiously, always keeping a quarter mile between themselves and the truck, the mares made their way to level ground, headed for the pond. The wind blew from behind them. Their wild manes and tails streamed forward and the scent of humans hurried ahead of them.

"Blackie's been doing this for years, Sam. He knows how to take care of himself."

Sam nodded, a little surprised Jake still thought of the stallion as Blackie, the colt she'd loved and lost.

Sam stayed quiet. She didn't want to frighten the mares. Still, she worried about her horse. Injured, he'd be prey for another stallion or coyotes. His own herd might outrun him.

"I've seen him up on the ridge," Sam whispered to Jake. "He stands guard between those wind-twisted pines while the mares drink."

Together they watched for the Phantom. Jake didn't approve of her obsession, but he knew that when she was worried about the stallion, nothing else mattered.

Sam was about to suggest they douse the headlights, when suddenly the Phantom was there.

Up on the ridge, moonlight struck his coat, turning it bright as liquid silver. The wind tossed his mane around his neck and shoulders.

"He looks fine," Jake said.

"No, he doesn't."

The stallion's head wasn't high flung and eager. He held it level with his shoulders. Though his ears pricked forward, alert, he rocked awkwardly as he took steps toward the path.

"Left rear leg?" Jake asked, as the stallion came down the mountain.

"Yes, just at the fetlock. I think some sagebrush stabbed him. Jake, he's really hurting. Look at him."

Head angled toward the truck, the stallion hobbled toward the pond.

Jake drew a breath, surprised that the stallion passed so much closer than the mares. Sam felt sure the Phantom had scented her.

She wanted to get out of the truck and go to him, but she let him drink. The water was cooling his injury.

"He's favoring that leg, but I don't think he's sick, yet." Jake leaned nearer the windshield. "I bet it could be swabbed clean, disinfected, and—oh no." Jake's head snapped Sam's way as if he'd heard her thoughts.

"Tell me, Jake. I'm going out there. You can help me or not, but I'm going."

"Don't dare me, or I'll drive away from here so fast it'll make your head spin."

"You won't," she insisted, "because it's not the right thing to do. Because you might be responsible for his death."

"Better his than yours."

"Will you get over that?" Sam didn't mean to shout, but she must have. The stallion's head left the water's surface so quickly, moisture scattered like diamonds.

"I am over it," Jake said. "That doesn't mean you shouldn't be careful."

"Of course I'll be careful. I'll get out of the truck, walk toward him, and if he wants my help—and he *has* before—I'll look at his fetlock."

"And then what?"

"If there's, like, something sticking out, I'll pull it loose."

"And leave him with an open wound? An invitation to infection? Great plan, Sam."

"No." Sam pressed her hands palm down on the purple first aid kit. "I'll use whatever you tell me to, from this."

Jake's breath rushed out. He muttered, "No, no, no." At the same time, he started assembling what she'd need.

"Listen to every word, Sam."

"I will." She watched him, knowing her mind had never been more alert. "But, remember, I can't carry too much. He always watches my hands. And I don't think he'll like this coat."

As Sam shrugged out of her sheepskin coat, Jake rubbed his forehead, but he didn't give in to frustration. He lifted the purple lid slowly, so the hinges wouldn't creak.

"We'll drench this gauze with water," Jake said, reaching to the truck floor to shake a plastic water bottle. "Good thing you didn't finish yours. If he lets you close enough, go to his near side and face back, toward his tail, to clean that wound."

"Facing back? Are you sure?"

"I'm—" Jake hesitated. One other time he'd been sure, and caused her accident. "I think his kick would have the least strength from that position."

"I'll do it. What next?"

Sam listened, shoving gauze and a needleless syringe of betadine into her pockets. Last, she tucked a disposable diaper—a perfect lightweight bandage—into her jeans' waistband.

Before she could climb out, the Phantom summoned her.

"Jake, look."

The Phantom limped toward the truck. He left the mares behind and halted about four car lengths away to stand in the headlights' beam. He tossed his head in three quick jerks and stood, ears swiveled toward her. Then, looking right at her, he nickered.

"If I get out now, he won't run." Sam put her hand on the truck door, then stopped. The Phantom trusted her to do what was right. "Is this all I need, Jake?"

"I'm trying to think—" Jake rubbed the back of his neck. "Aw shoot, it can't hurt. Here,"

Confused, Sam watched as Jake reached into their sandwich sack and sorted out a small piece of plain bread. "My grandfather used to make bread poultices for horses. To draw out infection, he said."

"Bread," Sam repeated.

As Jake dampened the bread with water, Sam listened to his directions, but she kept watching the Phantom.

"Do you know what's going to happen to me, if

you get hurt?" Jake muttered.

His words wrenched her attention away from the stallion.

Sam bristled with anger. "I know I'm getting really sick of you expecting me to fail," she said and scooted toward the door.

"No, I don't think you'll fail, or I wouldn't let you go," Jake snarled. Sam saw Jake really didn't care if they kept fighting. "Now, get him back in the water."

"What?" Sam barely got the word out. Jake couldn't change the rules at the last minute.

"You tamed him in the water. He trusts you in the water." Jake's voice was level and calm. "Get him back in the water or the deal is off."

Forget it, Sam thought. She opened the truck door as silently as she could. Then she glanced back.

"My hand's going to be on the horn," Jake said, demonstrating. "If the safest thing for you is to scare him away, I'll lean on this horn with everything I've got."

Jake and his idiot caution.

Sam moved toward the pond. The mares scattered further up the hillside, but the Phantom stayed quiet. As she passed, his head bobbed, scattering his mane and forelock free of his brown eyes. His weight rested on his three good legs. Maybe that, and pain, made it hard for Sam to read his body language.

Would he follow? He hadn't since he was a colt.

The sound of following hooves did not come. Sam

glanced back over her shoulder. Every line of the stallion's body showed his puzzlement. Whenever he'd come to her before, she'd met him. Now, she was walking away.

"Come on, boy." Sam swung along at a casual pace.

Icy water slapped over her tennis shoes and soaked her socks. She waded out three steps, four, five . . . and heard the splash of hooves behind her.

Yes. Sam felt a smile lift her lips. This stallion was the most wonderful horse in the world. Sam wanted to throw her arms around his satiny neck, but when she turned the night wind pierced her tee shirt. The chill was like a splash of cold water, awakening her to the fact that this was no dream.

The stallion was curious but cautious. He whuffled his lips, switched his tail, then stamped a forefoot. When he stamped, his balance shifted and he stumbled a step.

"Poor boy."

The stallion sighed as Sam edged closer. She held her hands out to him. Up the hillside, the clustered mares raised their heads. The stallion sniffed her hands, then turned his attention to her pockets and waistband. Maybe he couldn't see the supplies she'd hidden, but he knew they were there.

"We haven't done this in a long time, boy." Sam walked past the horse's front legs, dragging her hand along his sleek hide. "I'm going back here, okay? I'll pet you as I go, so you know right where I am. Full hand, okay, boy? No tickly stuff."

He kept the injured leg clear of the water. Sam half squatted and he allowed it. "Good, good boy."

He let her touch his fetlock. Just as Sam realized it felt hot, he jerked away from her shaking hand. She tried again and he let her dab at the wound with the gauze.

Sam had faced his tail, just as Jake ordered, but now she looked over her shoulder. The Phantom was watching. He blinked, looking nervous, but no more than a domestic horse would.

Sam hurried. Once the hair was washed free of dirt, she noticed a nub of sagebrush protruding from the wound. Why hadn't she brought tweezers?

Sam's knees shook, but she kept her hands steady. She knew what she had to do.

"This is the test," she crooned to the horse. "I'll get it right the first time, but it's going to hurt. Zanzibar, good boy, just let me do it and you'll be better."

Using her fingernails like tweezers, she jerked the sagebrush free. *Don't honk, don't honk*, Sam thought, and Jake didn't, though the stallion bolted a splashing step forward.

The Phantom stopped, shuddering.

"That was the hard part, boy."

Sam edged back into position. The stallion's head swung back and nuzzled her shoulder. He didn't want her facing away. She let him lip her shirt, hoping it would distract him when she squirted a stream of disinfectant on the wound.

His skin shivered, but he didn't move away.

"The medicine's just cold, right, boy?" Sam's own teeth were about to chatter, but it had nothing to do with the temperature.

Fingers flying, she molded the damp bread against the stallion's fetlock, glad he held the hoof above the water. The Phantom seemed to relax.

"You like that, boy? It's supposed to draw out the infection. That's what Jake's grandpa said. You remember Jake, don't you?"

The stallion didn't respond and he didn't trust the disposable diaper. At the first crinkle of plastic, his ears flattened. He walked out of the water, and this time Sam followed. Jake had better not honk. The disposable diaper and the pond water were a lousy combination. He ought to have the sense to see that.

Once out of the water, the stallion circled back. Clearly irritated, he swung his head in her direction and snapped his teeth.

"'Just get it over with,' is that it, boy?" Sam kept her voice low and worked quickly.

She pressed the bread poultice more firmly into place, wrapped the plastic diaper around the stallion's leg and fastened the tapes.

As her fingers left his leg, the stallion launched himself away. By the time Sam regained her feet, he was gone.

Sam got the truck door open. She sat in the doorway, unlaced her shoes and poured out the water, and stripped off her socks. By the time she closed the door, Sam was shaking so hard, she couldn't get arms into her coat sleeves. Once she quit struggling, she noticed Jake's silence.

"Didn't you even watch?" she asked.

"I watched."

Sam waited, excitement fading. "Wasn't it incredible?"

"He remembers you, I guess."

"Why are you talking like a robot?" Sam asked.

"I'll stop." Jake started the truck and drove back toward the main road.

Sam crossed her legs and wiggled one bare and freezing foot. It seemed unlikely that Jake was waiting for a compliment, but she gave one anyway. "Everything you told me to do worked."

Jake just kept driving.

By the time the truck tires bounced off the dirt road and back onto the asphalt, Jake still hadn't spoken.

"Why are you acting so weird?" Sam demanded.

Jake looked over. His expression mirrored the Phantom's as he'd pinned his ears back and glared.

"I hate feeling afraid," Jake said as if she'd dragged the words out of him. "Half the time I'm around you—"

He didn't finish. He waved one hand in dismissal

and leaned closer to the steering wheel.

Sam let him drive. He'd only had his license a month and it was a bad idea to distract him.

His reaction wasn't a surprise. Her accident had changed their friendship.

Sam tugged her coat cuffs down and pulled her fingers up into her sleeves. She didn't want Jake to worry, but she wasn't going to sit home playing Nintendo or doing her nails either.

Facing forward, Sam rolled her eyes to peer at him. The dashboard lights glowed off the shelf of his cheekbones and lit his hard-set jaw.

Let him sit there, Sam thought. *She* sure wouldn't talk first.

River Bend's porch light was visible miles before they crossed the bridge and rolled into the ranch yard.

Sam had hopped down from the truck and started to close the door when Jake's voice stopped her.

"Here's Mom's camera."

He dangled it by a leather strap and Sam wanted to refuse. Why hadn't he given it to her earlier, when they were on the range with the horses? That had been the plan.

As she took the camera, Sam felt an odd satisfaction. Jake hadn't forced it on her earlier, because he'd known she was watching for the Phantom.

"See ya at school," she said through a tight throat.

"Yeah," Jake sounded resigned. "I'll see ya."

❦

Sam was asleep when the telephone rang downstairs in the kitchen. With a half-formed idea that it was Jen, Sam swung her feet to the floor and raised her nightgown hem so she wouldn't trip. She ran down the stairs, vaguely aware of Dad lumbering along behind her.

Sam had reached the kitchen when Dad spoke. "I'll get that," he said. "Get on back to bed."

Sam let Dad lift the receiver.

"Hello," he said, but nothing in Dad's expression told her who'd called so late. She moved slowly, listening. Near the top of the stairs, she heard half a sentence.

"—businesswoman would have an answering machine."

Businesswoman? The only businesswomen she knew lived in San Francisco.

Curiosity on the boil, Sam sat on the top step.

". . . wanted poster . . . stallion . . ." Dad's voice rose, then faded. He had to be talking about Slocum and the Phantom.

Like a latch clicking into place, she knew it must be Brynna Olson.

Sam tiptoed back to her room, mulling over that possibility. Was Brynna back already? Did anyone go from Nevada to Washington, D. C. for a single day?

No.

And Washington's time was three hours ahead of

Nevada's. Sam rolled back into bed. Why would Brynna call Dad so late at night?

Brynna calling Dad. Sam stared at her bedroom ceiling until she saw a haze of spots, feathery horses and flying arrows.

Brynna could be urging Dad to take that job. Dad might have left a message with the Willow Springs office about Slocum's posters. Or maybe . . .

Sam flopped over and buried her face in her pillow.

Maybe she needed to go into Darton and see a movie before her imagination ran away from her completely.

Chapter Seventeen ❧

Sam's HEAD SNAPPED back, and her eyelids sprung wide as Dad braked at the bus stop.

"I don't want you falling asleep in class now," Dad cautioned.

"I won't," Sam promised.

She felt cranky. She'd asked Dad about his talk with Brynna, but Dad only said Brynna was gone for a week of meetings.

Since Jen wasn't at the bus stop yet and Sam didn't want to wait alone, she tried once more to lever information out of him.

"Exactly what did she say about Slocum's posters?"

Dad thought a minute, then recited, "Soon as someone at Willow Springs heard about the posters, they should've had a ranger call on Slocum to educate him about the Wild Horse and Burro Act."

Again, Sam thought. She'd been sitting next to Slocum when Brynna had explained it the first time.

Slocum knew he was breaking the law. He just didn't care.

"Can they arrest him?" Sam asked.

Dad didn't sugarcoat the truth. "Nope, not until something happens to the animal."

As soon as Jen arrived at the bus stop, she told Sam the stallion had been sniffing around Gold Dust Ranch the night before.

"My dad thinks he's come back for Kitty," Jen said as the bus arrived.

Once they were seated, Sam looked at Jen and decided to trust her with the truth.

"Jake and I saw the Phantom last night," Sam whispered. "He's hurt. So it couldn't have been him."

Jen sat up so suddenly, her glasses slipped down her nose. If intelligence could show in someone's expression, Jen's blue eyes glittered with brainpower.

"He's hurt?" Jen whispered. "If you don't want to call the BLM to take care of him, I could help." Jen's heart was set on becoming a veterinarian.

"I wish you had been there last night," Sam said. "But I think he's going to be all right."

Sam's mind churned. She had Mrs. Ely's camera around her neck. If Hammer really had been at the Gold Dust Ranch, he might come back tonight. If she were there, she could prove her point right away.

Sam had just drawn a breath to test her plan on Jen, when a boy's shout cut her off.

"Look at those idiots!"

Every student on the bus watched a black truck swerve across the range, raising a rooster's tail of dust. A skinny, shirtless guy stood in the truck bed, hugging the cab for balance. A lariat dangled from his hand, but he was hanging on too hard to use it.

"They're chasing a horse," Jen said, pointing. "It must be for the reward. Look, the truck has Idaho license plates."

But Sam couldn't look away from the horse. Long-limbed and root-beer colored, he raced toward the school bus. Their driver slowed to let him pass.

As he did, Sam noticed the animal wasn't young. His muzzle was gray and the bridge of his nose had been rubbed bare by years of wearing a bridle.

"He's not even wild," Sam gasped.

"He looks like an old saddle horse someone turned out after years of ranch work," Jen agreed. "Some reward."

"I'm phoning the BLM as soon as I get to school," Sam said.

"Your dad already did," Jen reminded her. "It didn't do any good."

Although Sam blamed the men in the black truck for their actions, Slocum had created this craziness by dangling a reward.

"I'm calling the BLM again," Sam insisted as the truck drove out of sight. "And I won't hang up until someone listens."

Jen nodded, then withdrew a pen from her backpack, grabbed Sam's hand and began writing on it.

"What's that?" Sam asked.

"The truck's license number." Jen shrugged at Sam's amazement. "Numbers just stick in my brain."

Things could go wrong in such a hurry.

As soon as Sam arrived at school, she jogged to the journalism room. Mr. Blair let her use his telephone and listened while she talked.

After she reported the men harassing the horse, an efficient voice at the Willow Springs holding pens thanked Sam and explained a ranger had already been dispatched to deal with the situation.

Sam's next ugly chore was to tell Mr. Blair about the camera. He didn't seem shocked. In fact, Mr. Blair was almost sympathetic as he looked the camera over and agreed with Mrs. Ely's diagnosis of a broken mirror.

"You'll have to pay for the repair," he said. "But it shouldn't be more than a couple hundred dollars."

Before Sam could hit the floor in a faint, Mr. Blair explained how she would go about earning money to pay for the repair. That's when Sam felt the icy fingers of panic.

"One of those sandwiches and one package of — no, two packages of corn chips."

Halfway through her first shift in Darton High

School's snack bar, Sam had reached three conclusions.

One, teenagers really did have lousy diets.

Two, she must earn good grades and attend college to avoid long-term snack bar employment.

Three, if another dollar bill stamped with Rachel's name smeared pink ink on her hands, she would scream.

This was Mr. Blair's remedy for penniless wrongdoers. She worked in the school snack bar but never saw a dollar of her wages. The Darton High bookkeeper deposited Sam's pay directly into the school newspaper's bank account.

Sam stared through the order window, trying to enjoy the sunlight and forget tomorrow's algebra test.

The job wasn't too bad. Jen had come by to sympathize and so had Jake's friend Darrell, though he was mostly interested in negotiating a deal on sunflower seeds. That meant Jake would know about her humiliation soon.

All at once, her view of the school courtyard vanished.

"Samantha Forster." Rachel strained to put a British slant on the name. "Whatever are you doing here?"

Sam couldn't think of a clever answer, so she extended a cellophane wrapped dessert.

"Want a Ding Dong, Rachel?" Sam thought how appropriate it was that she'd been basking in the sunshine streaming through the snack bar window until Rachel blocked it.

"What I want is for you to explain why a ranger showed up at my house this morning." Rachel's expressive hands reminded Sam of rosy talons.

"Hurry," urged a voice from behind Rachel. "The bell's gonna ring in a minute and—"

Rachel swung to face the impatient customer.

"Do you mind?" Her icy tone sent the boy running.

Sam looked after the guy, grateful he'd distracted Rachel.

"Go ahead and play innocent," Rachel snarled when Sam didn't speak. "But you've declared war on the wrong family. You have no idea how unpleasant your life will be, if you decide to stick around." Then, she flounced off without buying a thing.

Sam and Rachel ignored each other during journalism. In fact, the newspaper staff labored toward a deadline in near silence. The only sounds were tapping computer keys and rustling paper.

Three minutes before class ended, Mr. Blair approached Sam. She braced herself for the possibility the camera was ruined.

"Forster, are you still interested in night shoots?" he asked.

Night shoots. Sam's relief was so great, it took her a few seconds to understand. Then she nodded vigorously.

"Do you think I can do them with this?" Sam held up Mrs. Ely's old Pentax.

"Sure. It'd be easier with one of those little point-and-shoot jobs you see on television, but you wouldn't learn anything.

"Quick lesson." Mr. Blair glanced at the clock. "Listen up."

As he explained, Sam took notes on the back of an algebra worksheet. The grade on the front side wasn't worth saving.

Most of Mr. Blair's directions made sense. She hoped she understood enough to carry out the plan she and Jen had put together.

Sam checked her watch and counted. In four hours, she should be arriving to study algebra and spend the night at Jen's house. In five-and-a-half hours, Jen's parents should be driving off for their weekly "date" in Darton. Just after that, Sam would be crouched and ready for the blue stallion's appearance.

A day or two later, she figured, she'd be rich.

"Hey, Forster, no daydreaming." Mr. Blair snapped his fingers. "Don't be afraid to *shoot*. Film comes out of the factory by the mile, so keep shooting as long as there's something to see."

The bell shrilled, class ended, and Sam rushed out. She needed to find Jen and work out a few more details.

◖◗

They spent so long conspiring at the bus stop, Sam and Jen both had to jog home before someone came looking for them.

Dressed in jeans and a white blouse, with her hair in a tidy knot, Gram waited for Sam at the door.

"What did your teacher say about the camera?" Gram asked.

Sam explained and prepared to launch her plan, but when she entered the house, she was nearly sidetracked. A meringue-topped lemon pie sat on the kitchen table.

She loved lemon meringue pie and Gram knew it. Since Sam had worked through the lunch hour, she was hungry. She could almost taste the sugary meringue and lemon tartness on her tongue.

But some things were more important than food. Like saving her horse. Sam turned her back on the pie and met Gram's eyes.

"Gram, I got a C minus on my algebra pretest today." Sam saw Gram wince. "Tomorrow is the real test, and Jen offered to help me study. I know it's a school night, but numbers just come naturally to her and I really need the help."

"Why didn't you girls get together right after school?" Gram asked.

"I had my chores to do." Sam gestured toward the pasture and barn. Though Buddy's brand and Ace's bites were almost healed, Sam still checked them. And of course there were chickens to tend and water troughs to check. "So can I please spend the night?"

"I guess it wouldn't hurt," Gram said, "if you two don't stay up too late."

"We still have to catch the bus in the morning," Sam said and Gram nodded. Sam figured she could sleep in this weekend.

If there was a truer test of friendship, Sam couldn't imagine it. Jen offered to help Sam study the material for her algebra test. Instead, Jen ended up teaching.

"You really don't get this, do you?" Jen was mystified.

"I really don't, but you make more sense than any teacher I've had so far."

"Cool," Jen said. "Wait until you see me on linear equations."

At last, Sam declared her brain was full, so the girls baked frozen pizza and drank sodas. After washing the dishes, they picked the perfect spot for Sam and her camera.

The sorrel mare, Kitty, had been trotting along the fence since dusk. Her high-strung actions convinced the girls Hammer was near.

"I know it will work," Jen said. "It's not like you're trying to catch him, just photograph him. What can go wrong?"

"Your parents could come home early."

"They won't," said Jen. "Statistically speaking, it cannot happen. My parents are creatures of habit."

Because she planned to be tucked up inside the house watching television while Sam shivered behind a stump, Jen refused to share the reward money. She did agree to let Sam buy her a poster of her hero, mathematician and scientist Albert Einstein, if everything went as planned.

Now, Sam crouched next to Kitty's corral, reviewing Mr. Blair's advice on shooting in the darkness. When she tired of that, Sam watched Kitty. She couldn't ignore the Phantom's mother.

Clean-limbed and graceful, Kitty trotted around the corral, then stopped a few feet from Sam. When Kitty cocked her head to the side, as if wondering what Sam was up to, a lock of flaxen mane veiled one eye.

Sam smooched at the mare. Kitty's ears flickered back and forth, then she struck at the dirt with a foreleg. Sam had seen the Phantom do the very same thing. Had he learned it from his mom? When Kitty lived at River Bend, she and her son had shared the same pasture for two years.

As the mare sidled near, Sam reached out. Kitty shied and bolted across the corral.

"Hey, girl," Sam said. "Don't be afraid."

Seconds later, Kitty returned, alert ears turned to catch Sam's voice.

"Your baby's turned out real nice," Sam told the inquisitive mare. "He's a stallion with pretty colts of his own. You'd be proud of him."

Sam tried to shake off a wave of sadness. She needed to look through the camera's viewfinder. This was no time to let her eyes blur with tears simply because she missed her own mother.

The next time Kitty shied, Sam hadn't moved a muscle.

It must be him. The sorrel's head lifted. Her nostrils sampled the wind. Kitty stared into the darkness. Sam followed her stare but saw nothing. The mare snorted. Her legs were braced straight as broomsticks. Something was there.

A hoof clacked on asphalt. The Shetlands near the front gate moved across the frosty grass, and nickers floated on night air.

Hammer, Sweetheart, and Apache Hotspot drifted like ghosts up the driveway.

Patience. Let them get closer, Sam told herself. Her fingers trembled. She'd done everything Mr. Blair suggested, except brace the camera against something solid. For that, she'd have to wait until the horses moved into position.

The blue looked sleeker than before. Jets of steam huffed from his nostrils. His massive head swung from side to side, checking each shadow in the ranch yard.

Hammer didn't move as if his fight with the Phantom had lamed him. With rippling stealth the blue stallion drew closer, looking prehistoric and tough.

His shoulders churned as he came on. Ranch

lights glimmered on wisps of hair under his chin, making the stallion look like a bearded unicorn. Sam remembered how Hammer had turned on her, treating her as an enemy, threatening to run her down just before the Phantom appeared. She didn't look forward to startling him.

Tonight, the Phantom couldn't save her. If the blue stallion heard the click of the shutter, he'd be in her face or gone.

Just a few feet away sat a series of flat-topped redwood hitching posts with brass rings. As the stallion passed the farthest one, Sam thought she might use the nearest one to prop her camera.

Almost there. Almost . . .

Far out, car headlights slashed across the desert. The electric gates whirred, responding to a remote-control opening the entrance to the Gold Dust Ranch.

Hammer hesitated and Sam knew what she had to do.

She ran into the stallion's path. He reared. Click. He threatened her with his fury. Click.

Sam braced against the redwood post, following the rising torso and flailing forefeet. Then, as the Kenworthys' headlights lit the horses from behind, Sam took a final shot of the rearing stallion with the red-eyed mares behind him.

She expected the stallion to turn and run. Instead, he bolted straight toward her. Flint-hard hooves reached forward, pulling his body after. Sam ducked behind the redwood post, and rolled to the ground, clutching Mrs. Ely's camera to her chest.

Eyes wide open, she saw the shaggy belly pass overhead. She heard the crash of his hooves landing, running past Sam, past Kitty, past Slocum's mansion on the hill, and into the night.

Chapter Eighteen ❧

SATURDAY MORNING, two days after Sam's photograph ran on page one of the Darton *Review-Journal*, the newspaper still sat on kitchen table.

ROGUE STALLION REVEALED! shouted the headline.

While Jake and Dad fought to read the follow-up article in today's newspaper, Sam ate the cinnamon toast Gram had just served and studied her picture again.

In rearing close-up, Hammer looked like a Wild West bronco. The mares behind him looked terrified. She almost wished the stallion captured on film had been the Phantom. At least it would mean he was alive.

It had been three days since she'd seen him, wounded and limping. Her amateurish vet care might not have been enough to save him from infection.

Sam shook her head against her gloomy thoughts

and straightened the wrinkles in the newspaper. She'd studied the picture so often, it hardly seemed to be hers anymore, but the tiny type under the photograph read, PHOTO BY S. FORSTER.

Sam remembered how Mr. Blair had interrupted Mrs. Ely's history class to show Sam the picture as soon as he'd developed her film.

Mr. Blair and Mrs. Ely had encouraged Sam to submit the photograph to the *Review-Journal*. They'd claimed the recognition would build her self-esteem, but Sam knew the truth. The teachers thought Linc Slocum would try to wriggle out of paying the reward.

That's exactly what he was doing.

The newspaper across the table rustled fiercely as Jake demanded their attention.

"Listen to this," Jake said, reading. "'The reward of ten thousand dollars has yet to be paid. According to local rancher Lincoln Slocum, who offered the reward, "My posters clearly state the reward will be paid for the stallion's capture and information leading to Apache Hotspot's return. The filly is still out on the range. As far as I'm concerned, after running with that wild bunch, she can stay there."'"

Gram, Dad, and Jake grumbled in disapproval.

Sam had another hope, though. She'd heard a helicopter making sweeps overhead all morning. Perhaps the BLM was on the stallion's trail.

"Never thought I'd be glad to hear those choppers," Dad echoed Sam's thought. "But that son of a gun Slocum owes you a college fund."

"And Sweetheart should be back here where she belongs," Gram said.

"I just want to hear Slocum tell Sam thank you." Jake laughed.

"But he is right." Sam went to the refrigerator for the pitcher of orange juice. "He— I'll get it."

Sam broke off when the phone rang.

"Good morning, Samantha. This is Brynna Olson. Sorry to call so early—"

"Brynna? When did you get back?" Sam looked up. Jake met her eyes and began punching the air. He must think Brynna could force Slocum to pay up. Sam crossed her fingers.

"Yesterday. And I bet you can guess what I found on my desk when I went in to work."

"The newspaper?"

"Yesiree." Brynna's voice sounded young and completely unprofessional. "Congratulations on that super photograph and on snagging the reward."

"But, well . . ." Sam's voice faltered. She didn't want to drain away Brynna's excitement. "In today's paper, he says—" Sam broke off, realizing Brynna wasn't listening.

"What are you doing for lunch today?" Brynna asked. "Do you think you could make it to Clara's in Alkali about noon?"

"I'll see." Sam felt awkward as she turned to Dad. "I don't quite understand what's going on, but

Brynna is" — Sam spun her hand next to her head — "pretty excited. In fact, she's downright giddy and she wants us to meet her at Clara's today at noon."

Dad drained his coffee cup and set it down hard. His face held no more expression than the tabletop as he said, "Tell her we'll be there."

Sam stared in amazement. Saturday was a serious workday on the River Bend Ranch. They never went out for lunch. Something was going on.

"Brynna? Dad says we'll be there."

"I don't suppose Clara serves champagne," Brynna said, laughing.

"What?" Sam wondered what had happened to Brynna in Washington.

"Never mind, just plan on chocolate upside-down cake for everyone. And, Sam, you know what?"

Sam was almost afraid to ask, but curiosity won out. "What?"

"It'll be your treat."

The blue stallion didn't enjoy the party held in his honor. He kicked the tailgate of the horse trailer parked in front of Clara's café.

Inside, the jukebox played, and Clara dealt out plates of cheeseburgers and fries to the table of rowdy customers celebrating Sam's victory.

But Sam stood over by the window, beside a young woman watching the horse trailer.

Rosa Perez had midnight hair and the flavor of

New Mexico in her voice.

"He is such a bad boy." Rosa tried to glimpse the horse inside the trailer, then turned to Sam with a smile. "And I am so glad to be taking him home."

Sam's photograph had helped the BLM capture the horses from a ravine on the other side of Lost Canyon.

Now, Apache Hotspot and Sweetheart were back in their home corrals. And even before the horses were found, Brynna's first look at Sam's picture convinced her he was no mustang.

One phone call and a risky peek at the tattoo inside his upper lip verified it. "Hammer" was the California endurance champion Brynna had heard about by e-mail weeks ago. Within hours, Rosa Perez had started driving to Willow Springs to be reunited with her beloved Diablo.

"I hope he didn't cause you any harm," Rosa said now. "I know he has a bad habit of charging."

Sam pictured the horse bearing down on her, ears pinned back, but she only shook her head.

"I bought him from a logger, who used him for pulling and, I think, whipped him a lot." Rosa looked back at the trailer and smiled. "He's mild as a dove with me."

"Some horses just bond with one person," Sam said, understanding.

She gazed at the road beyond the horse trailer. Any minute now, Linc Slocum was supposed to arrive with a check, making everything perfect.

All the same, Sam wasn't as happy as she should be. She missed the Phantom.

Since she'd bandaged his fetlock, there'd been no sign of the mustang. Sam tried to think positively, but she couldn't stop worrying.

Laughter boomed from the table where Jake, Gram, Dad, and Brynna sat talking. Applause greeted a tray of Clara's chocolate upside-down cake.

Everyone was having fun, but Sam wouldn't really celebrate until she'd seen her horse, whole and healthy. The quickest way to do that was retrace her steps to the Phantom's haven. Soon. It was only August, but the high pass and stone tunnel leading to the wild horse hideout could be blocked by an early snow.

"Sam! Come eat!" Jake held up a plate of cake.

"In a minute," she said. Sam noticed Dad had a little smear of chocolate next to his mouth. If she timed it right, maybe he'd say yes when she asked to return to the Phantom's home. Of course, that meant telling him about it.

From outside the café, Sam heard the blare of country-Western music. She and Rosa squinted at sun glaring off the beige Cadillac. Slocum had arrived.

"Oh my," Rosa said.

Linc Slocum heaved himself free of the car and straightened the coat of his Western-style suit. The suit was purple as plum jam, but his Stetson was white and he wore a bolo tie set off by a polished rock.

Although neither Sam nor Rosa could hear what he said, they saw Slocum lean toward the horse trailer and speak to the stallion.

Diablo kicked the tailgate of his trailer with renewed vigor. Rosa reached into her purse for her car keys.

"Thank you, again, Samantha, for everything." Rosa gave Sam a hug that said more than words. "I think I must leave before my endurance horse can endure no more."

Rosa waved and slipped through the café door. As Slocum tipped his Stetson after Rosa, Sam hurried back to the table and plopped into the chair next to Jake's.

"Mr. Slocum." Dressed in her khaki uniform, Brynna greeted the rancher strutting toward them.

Sam uncrossed her arms and legs. A second later, she realized she'd crossed them again. Slocum had an oblong piece of paper in his hand. It was really going to happen.

"Hello, folks," he said. "I figured—"

Slocum blushed. All his bluster was costing him a small fortune. Sam tried to feel sorry for Slocum, but she couldn't.

"That is, Miss Samantha—"

Then, Jake caught Sam's eye. In a subtle movement, Jake rubbed the side of his neck, reminding

Sam of the Phantom's scar. Sam straightened in her chair and met Slocum's bashful expression with a glare.

Since Slocum couldn't pay the stallion for the pain he'd inflicted, the next best thing was paying someone who loved him.

"Yes, Mr. Slocum?" Sam stood.

"Well, I know Wyatt is just as happy as a dog with two tails to wag, so I won't take up your time. Thanks for finding that filly of mine and getting her home, uh, safe."

Sam knew why Slocum hesitated over the last word. The vet who'd checked the animals after capture suspected Hotspot was in foal.

Slocum ran his fingers through his slicked-back hair until it stuck out at odd angles. "In fact," he said with a short laugh, "I may just insist you take a bonus with your reward check. How 'bout you keep one stall open, Wyatt? This baby may not fit in with my Appaloosa breeding program. Still, with those two for parents, you might end up with a colt who's fast as a caged squirrel."

As those around her laughed, Sam took the check. This skinny piece of paper would pay Mr. Blair for the camera, put in new fence rails where Diablo had broken them, and replace River Bend's aged pump. Dad was making her save the rest for college, but she planned to keep back a few dollars for a present.

Jake looked over in surprise as Sam squeezed his hand. She couldn't help thinking about his October first birthday and the beautiful bridle just waiting in Tully's Western Wear.

Frost clung like silver icing to every twig and branch, as Sam rode Ace away from the Calico Mountain camp the next morning. An early cold snap made frozen brush sparkle as the sun rose. It was all the more beautiful because Jake had let her come alone.

Trusting her, even though she wouldn't tell exactly where she was going, Dad had allowed Jake to drive Sam back to the Phantom's territory. He'd instructed Jake to let her approach the stallion's secret haven alone.

Sam checked her watch. It was five A.M.

Jake had driven to the site where they'd held the herd the night she and Ace had been kidnapped by the Phantom. As soon as they'd arrived and unloaded the horses, Jake had built a campfire, positioned his sleeping bag next to it, then crawled inside.

Leaning on one elbow, he'd rattled off orders.

"You've got two hours to get there and get back, or I'm coming after you," Jake insisted. "Witch can catch your old pony without even trying."

Sam was counting on Ace to help find the mustangs' hideout. Everything looked different than it had in early summer.

A crystal forest of cottonwood trees crowded around her and the broad plain seemed smaller. Was Ace taking a different approach to the stone tunnel and wild valley?

The footing turned steep. That seemed right. Sam recalled shale shaped like dinner plates, but she didn't see it as they climbed upward.

Sam kept her weight balanced, sparing Ace. The little mustang snorted and looked from side to side, more watchful than ever.

"Do we need the Phantom to lead us back, boy?"

Ace shook his head so hard, the buckles on his headstall clinked. Sam loosened the reins, wishing the stallion would appear.

Fear hovered over her like a storm cloud. What if she found the way back and her horse wasn't there?

All at once, Sam saw the faint path Ace was following. It was no more than a dust smear through silver-green sagebrush. Though it ran along a cliff, Ace's delicate hooves navigated it with ease.

"Good boy," Sam whispered, and then she saw what the uncertain light had hidden. A steeper path climbed a cleft between two rocks, and suddenly they moved into darkness.

Ace stopped. His hooves echoed as he shifted from hoof to hoof on the slick rock, but he didn't go forward.

Sam listened. She dismounted, then ground-tied Ace, as if the act of holding the reins could distract her from something she must hear.

The tunnel turned from brown-gray to black just ahead.

"You stay, boy. I'll be back."

Sam walked into the gloom. She wouldn't think of bats, of earthquakes, of tons of stone hanging overhead.

The way ahead was silent. Cold shimmered from the walls. She could not hear the rushing stream in the Phantom's hidden valley, nor the squeals of hungry foals. She heard no hooves striking rock, telling her the stallion was coming to meet her.

Was she lost? Sam wrapped her arms around her waist, shrinking away from the narrowing stone walls. Could this be the wrong tunnel?

Up ahead, brightness flickered. Cheered as if sunlight warmed her, Sam recalled a crack in the tunnel roof. That must be it.

But it wasn't formless daylight. The pale shape wavered like a ghost.

Zanzibar?

It couldn't be. No matter how wild, no animal could move so silently. Then, she said the word aloud.

"Zanzibar."

In this lonely cavern, it must be safe to speak a secret name.

For a heartbeat, Sam blinked against the brightness,

and then her stallion stood before her, whole and healthy.

His front hooves lifted off the stone floor, spinning in a blur. He would have reared in greeting, if not for the low stone ceiling.

His back hooves pranced with no trace of a limp. *No limp.*

This time, Sam didn't think. She embraced his silvery neck and though the stallion lifted her briefly off her feet, he didn't run. He didn't flinch. He didn't bowl her over or neigh a protest.

The stallion stood, head over Sam's shoulder, chin moving up and down her spine, as if he hugged her, too.

"You're safe." Tears stung her eyes, but Sam blinked them away. She refused to miss an instant of magic.

It was a good thing, because Zanzibar leaped backward. Head tossing, he gave her chest a push. Off balance, Sam retreated a step. With the persistence of a father moving his child along, the stallion urged her back another step, toward Ace, still ground-tied and waiting.

Sam stepped backward, until Ace's whinny vibrated through the tunnel. For only a second, Sam looked behind her.

When she turned to face the stallion one last time, shadows had taken his place.

"He was here, Ace." Her voice echoed around her

and the gelding nickered in agreement.

Zanzibar was alive. He'd come back to tell her so.

As Sam walked out of the darkness, love bounded up in her like a fountain.

From

Phantom Stallion
৩ 3 ৩
DARK SUNSHINE

"Who wants fudge cake?" Gram asked.

Sam didn't moan. She resigned herself to believing this torture would never end.

Hands went up, including Mikki's. "I do, but please, can I run out to see if Popcorn will take a sugar cube from me? I'll be back before you serve dessert. I promise."

Since Gram always thought the best of everyone, Sam looked at Dad. He was watching Brynna smile at Mikki as if she hadn't noticed the girl smirking all through dinner.

"Hurry," Brynna said. "We'll wait for you."

Sam cleared dinner plates and wondered why she was the only one who heard phoniness in Mikki's voice. She rinsed the plates at the sink and looked toward the barn. She couldn't see Mikki.

Sam took a guilty glance toward Gram. Pleased at having company, Gram hummed as she sliced extra-thick slabs of cake.

Sam scolded herself. She'd promised to give

Mikki another chance, but she wasn't doing a very good job of it. She carried the cake plates to the table before Gram could ask.

Mikki returned right away, and if anyone else noticed that the girl reeked of cigarette smoke, they didn't say anything.

Why not? Sam knew that if Dad thought she'd smoked anywhere, let alone near the barn and horses, she'd be grounded for life.

Gram invited Brynna and Mikki to stay and watch television, or play Scrabble, but Brynna was already standing.

She looked uneasy, as if she'd just noticed Mikki's too-sweet temperament. Brynna sounded strained as she said good-bye and herded Mikki toward the door.

Dad beat her to it. With a gentlemanly bow, he opened the door, then stood there, blocking it.

He froze, hands gripping the doorframe.

"Wyatt?" Gram said. "What is it?"

Even then, Sam knew she'd never forget the awful despair in her father's voice.

"Oh, Lord, phone Luke Ely and have him call out the volunteers. The bunkhouse is on fire and the flames are reaching for the barn."

River Bend Ranch was burning.

Dad ran and Sam followed.

Black smoke corkscrewed into the evening sky. There wasn't much smoke yet. In fact, the yard was bright as noon and popping filled the air.

Sam hesitated in the middle of the yard and stared around. On her left, the horses in the ten-acre pasture ran in a tight, nervous herd. Ahead stood the barn, full of horses and winter's hay. No smoke. No fire.

She felt relieved, then even more relieved as she saw that Dad was right—black smoke came from the old bunkhouse.

Sam took off after Dad, and her relief ended the instant she came face-to-face with a sheet of orange flame three times taller than the ruined old building it consumed.

A wall of heat stopped her.

"Hose!" Dad shouted, and Sam jumped as he jerked the hose leading to the barn. It stretched behind him as he shot water on the blaze.

At least the old bunkhouse is empty. That's what Sam thought, until an arm of flame reached toward the barn and sparks peppered the air overhead.

Dark Sunshine began screaming. For days, the mare had pushed back her terror, trying to understand. Now the smoke and shouting and confinement freed her fear. The little buckskin whinnied for help, and Sam knew she'd lied to the horse. She'd told Dark Sunshine that she was all right, but nothing was all right.